## "Get down!"

Adam tackled her, knocking her flat in the mud as a bullet ricocheted a foot from Jaelyn's head.

"Go," he said.

She started a fast crawl over the carpet of leaves, twigs and rocks strewn over the boggy ground, keeping her body between the infant and the gunmen as she dragged the baby seat along beside her.

Another shot rang out, whipped through the bushes far too close for comfort. Adam took aim at two figures coming across the lawn toward them, and fired. One went down instantly, while his partner dived for the ground.

Adam took off. When he reached the far side of the parking lot, he searched for Jaelyn. He had no way of knowing if more men waited for them on this side of the building.

He stood, using a large pine tree for cover, and peeked around the trunk into the lot.

Headlights moved toward Adam, too fast to be a guest returning. He braced against the tree, aimed at the windshield...

# CHRISTMAS IN THE CROSSHAIRS

## DEENA ALEXANDER

**LOVE INSPIRED** SUSPENSE
INSPIRATIONAL ROMANCE

**LOVE INSPIRED® SUSPENSE**
INSPIRATIONAL ROMANCE

Recycling programs for this product may not exist in your area.

ISBN-13: 978-1-335-59779-3

Christmas in the Crosshairs

Copyright © 2023 by Denise Pysarchuk

For questions and comments about the quality of this book, please contact us at CustomerService@Harlequin.com.

Love Inspired
22 Adelaide St. West, 41st Floor
Toronto, Ontario M5H 4E3, Canada
www.LoveInspired.com

**Printed in U.S.A.**

Every good gift and every perfect gift is from above, and cometh down from the Father of lights, with whom is no variableness, neither shadow of turning.
—*James* 1:17

This book is lovingly dedicated to
my husband and children—you are my greatest blessings.

# ONE

"We're losing her!" Chaos erupted as two paramedics shoved a gurney through the emergency department doors at a dead run. One of them called out, "It's Jaelyn Reed. She was attacked."

Jaelyn's heart stuttered. She recognized the voice of her friend and fellow firefighter Pat Ryan. But what was he talking about? She was fine, just finishing up her Christmas Eve shift at the hospital, where she worked as a nurse when she wasn't volunteering as a firefighter for Seaport Fire and Rescue. Since she had no family to go home to, she often worked the holidays.

Footsteps pounded as doctors, nurses, and technicians rushed toward a commotion in one of the nearby cubicles.

She followed the sound of Pat's voice rattling off vitals down the corridor. Why had he said it was Jaelyn? That she'd been attacked? She'd known Pat Ryan since she was a kid, was friends with both him and his fiancée, Rachel, and she'd never heard the slightest edge of panic in his voice. Until now.

She stepped into the cubicle. "What's going on?"

Pat glanced at her then snapped his head back in a double take. "Jaelyn?"

"Pat, what happened?"

His gaze shot to the gurney, where a young woman lay unconscious as the nurses assessed and began treatment.

When Jaelyn followed his stare, her breath caught in her throat. Looking down at the woman's face was like looking into a mirror. The stranger shared the same long, nearly black hair as Jaelyn, though hers was tangled and matted with blood; the same delicate features, at least it appeared so beneath the contusions and swelling; and even the same slim, athletic build.

"I don't understand." Pat frowned and grabbed the woman's purse from the bottom of the gurney. "She looks enough like you to be your—"

"Sister." The one word escaped on a shallow huff of breath. Could this woman be her sister? The sister she hadn't even known existed until a month ago? It'd been almost a year since she'd taken the DNA test— just for fun, something she'd let her fellow firefighters convince her to do to pass the time amid a blizzard that had gripped the area last winter.

Jaelyn had grown up in Seaport, New York, a small town on the east end of Long Island's south shore, daughter of a prominent couple in the community, Dr. and Mrs. Elijah Reed. And she was an only child. The last thing she'd ever expected was to shake loose any deep, dark secrets from the Reed family tree. And then her results had come in…and last month the friends and family app had connected her to her twin. "Maya Barlowe."

"Yeah." Pat held out a slim photo holder with the woman's driver's license. The picture of the woman staring back at her could have been, well, her twin. "That's the name on her ID. Is she your sister?"

Apparently. Since Jaelyn's parents had been killed in a car accident five years ago, she hadn't been able to ask them about her. She had no other family—no one to lean on after her fiancé had left her for another woman while she was grieving—and she hadn't wanted to go to any of her parents' friends. At least, not yet. She'd needed time to process the information first. Jaelyn had yet to decide whether or not to reach out to the woman, try to ascertain how they shared not only the same DNA but the same birthdate as well. Even as she'd debated her options, she hadn't fully accepted the fact it could actually be true, that she could have a long-lost twin sister she'd never known about.

"Out of the way, guys." One of the other nurses shoved past her.

Coming to her senses, Jaelyn stepped aside, careful not to upset the delicate choreography as the doctors and nurses worked together in a desperate effort to save the woman's life.

Pat gripped her elbow and led her out into the hall-way. "Hey, you okay?"

Was she? She honestly didn't know. While she hated the thought of seeing anyone suffer, what was she sup-posed to feel for this woman who might be her twin but whom she'd never met? Confusion was the overwhelming emotion. She shoved a few stray strands of hair out of her face. "Yeah, I guess, but I don't understand what's going on. Where did you find her? And what happened to her?"

"A call came in." With a glance over his shoulder, Pat ushered her farther across the hall so they'd be out of the way. "A couple of kids riding dirt bikes came across her just before dusk in the woods behind the Seaport Bed and Breakfast. She'd been attacked, badly beaten. I'm sorry, Jaelyn, I didn't even know you'd reached out to her. I guess with the holidays and all..."

"No. That's the thing..." Only a handful of people knew about the secret Jaelyn's DNA test had revealed, Pat being one of them. Could someone she'd trusted have contacted Maya? No, not possible. The few close friends she'd told knew that Jaelyn wasn't sure how she wanted to handle the situation yet. None of them would have betrayed her confidence... Besides, she hadn't shared Maya's name with anyone. "I didn't reach out, nor did she contact me. I have no idea what she was doing here. I didn't even realize she knew about me."

"Assuming she's here because of you," Pat pointed out.

"I guess, but according to the information I have, she lives in New York City. What are the chances she just happened to show up a few miles from where I live and work?" Even though plenty of people from New York City visited the south shore of Eastern Long Island, especially around the holidays, most of them flocked to the Hamptons or Montauk. Seaport wasn't exactly a thriving tourist destination.

Pat frowned. "Slim to none, I'd say."

So her sister must have been trying to find her, which begged the question, why hadn't she tried to contact her? Or had she? Jaelyn had been on duty for the past twelve hours and hadn't bothered to check her messages. "My phone is in the locker room. I'll have to see if she tried to reach out."

"The police officers were questioning the kids who found her, but they'll be here any minute." He gestured in the direction of the locker room. "You should probably see if she tried to make contact before they get here. I'm sure they'll want to know if that's why she was in Seaport."

Dazed, Jaelyn paused and glanced into the cubicle where her coworkers and friends worked to save Maya. Should she go in? Try to help? Technically, she was off duty now, but still...

"There's nothing you can do for her in there, Jaelyn. She's being taken care of. It would probably help her more right now to find out if she tried to call you, if she left any kind of message, maybe indicated she was in trouble, anything that would help the police find who did this to her."

She nodded. He was right. "Yeah, okay."

"And Jaelyn..." He turned to face her, rubbed his hands up and down her arms. "I'm really sorry about your sister, but I'm glad you're okay. I'm not gonna lie, when we first arrived on scene and thought it was you, it gave both Jack and me a jolt."

She covered one of his hands with hers. "Thank you, Pat."

"Sure thing." Releasing her, he stuffed his hands into his pockets and started down the hall with her.

"You didn't check her ID there?" Jaelyn asked.

He only hesitated a fraction of a second, but it was a telling pause. "She's in bad shape, Jaelyn. We stabilized her and transported. Plus, like I said, we thought it was you, both recognized you immediately."

She nodded, understanding the urgency of the situation in that moment. Nothing but saving the patient would have mattered to the paramedics.

"I'll tell you what, I'll wait here and keep an eye on her while you go ahead and get your phone. You may as well get changed while you're in the locker room, so you can sit with your sister afterward."

She smiled at him, grateful he understood her need to know how Maya was doing. "Thank you."

"Of course." He squeezed her arm once more, as if needing to reassure himself she was fine. "I'll let the guys know you're okay."

She nodded and started toward the locker room at a brisk pace. Since she was not only a nurse in the emergency room, but also a volunteer firefighter and a member of a well-known family in the community, news of her being attacked would have spread quickly. Especially in the small town of Seaport. It would be good to squash the rumors before they could gain any real traction.

Thankfully, with Pat taking care of that, it was one less thing she had to worry about, and she could turn her attention to her sister. *Sister.* She still couldn't quite wrap her head around the idea. Being an only child was all she'd ever known. She shook off the confusion and increased her pace. None of that mattered now. The sooner she gathered her things, the sooner she could return to Maya and hopefully get some answers.

As she passed the nurses' station, a man's voice brought her up short. "I'm looking for Maya Barlowe?"

Jaelyn turned at the mention of her sister's name.

"Can you tell me if she was brought in—" A bulky man who had to be better than six feet tall shifted his attention from the nurses' station even as he asked the question. As he glanced in her direction, his gaze clashed with Jaelyn's. His expression showed confusion at first, but then it hardened and he straightened.

Jaelyn hesitated, caught off guard by the hostility marring his features.

His focus narrowed on her as he reached inside his jacket and pulled out a handgun.

Her breath caught in her lungs. A dull ache spread through her chest. Fear paralyzed her.

Eyes hard, hand dead steady, the man lifted the weapon toward her.

The chaos of the emergency department receded, and blackness tunneled her vision. It seemed nothing existed but the two of them caught in some deadly stare down. She desperately wanted to believe she was just in the wrong place at the wrong time, but her mind wouldn't allow her to accept that. The gunman's glare was too intense, his attention too pinpointed on her, and he'd just asked about her sister.

"Get down!" another man yelled.

Jaelyn couldn't react. All of her training as a nurse,

as a firefighter, had her remaining calm in the face of the weapon. It was the look in his eyes that had her blood running cold. She'd never seen such emptiness, such coldness, such…darkness.

And then someone tackled her from the side, even as the first bullets flew. Sheer terror swamped her.

More gunshots erupted. Screams, crashes, sobs tore through the emergency department as patients and staff ran or dove for cover, trying to protect those who were unable to flee.

Jaelyn landed hard on her elbow. Pain shot to her shoulder and her wrist, and her fingers went numb.

"Go, go, go!" The stranger half-dragged, half-shoved her toward an examination room door, knocking over the Christmas tree in an out-of-the-way corner.

Jaelyn scrambled in the direction she was led, hit the door at a crouch, and tumbled through.

Another round of gunshots pierced the air, too many for just the handgun she'd seen. Had the attacker had another weapon beneath his jacket, or was there a second gunman? Two shots shattered the window in the door.

Jaelyn covered her head and ducked against a row of cabinets.

"Stay down." The man who'd saved her lay a quick hand on her shoulder, glanced through the cracked window into the hallway and looked around.

His strong hand on her shoulder helped ground her. They had to get out of there. People needed help.

The gunman flung the door open and leveled what appeared to be an automatic weapon at Jaelyn.

"Oh, God, please help me." She closed her eyes as

she whispered the plea, prayed the attacker hadn't already harmed anyone, prayed he'd leave without killing anyone, then gathered her strength, coiled her muscles, and lunged at him.

A shot rang out beside her.

The gunman's eyes went wide as the bullet struck his chest, as if shocked someone had dared to shoot him, and he crumpled to the floor.

Jaelyn ignored the ringing in her ears, dropped to her knees at his side, and felt for a pulse.

The man who'd saved her caught her beneath the arm and hauled her to her feet. "We have to go. He won't be alone, and no one here will be safe until you're gone."

"What are you talking about?" Falling back on her training, she yanked her arm away and continued to triage, checking vitals, assessing damage.

"Listen to me." He crouched in front of her, lifted her chin until her gaze met his. Turmoil raged in his brown eyes, and his tawny hair was disheveled. "We have to go. Now."

"Look, I appreciate you saving me. Thank you. But I'm not going anywhere with you. I don't even know who you are. And I'm not leaving anyone to die." As she started chest compressions, Pat barreled through the door with his partner, Jack, on his heels.

Pat dropped beside her. "Are you all right?"

"I am, yes." Jack took over compressions, and Jaelyn used her wrist to swipe back a few strands of hair that had come loose from her ponytail. "Is anyone out there hurt?"

"Only minor injuries," Pat replied.

She offered up a prayer of thanks, knowing how much worse the outcome could have been. With Pat and Jack working to save the gunman, she slid out of the way and climbed to her feet, then met her stranger's angry expression with one of her own. "Explain. Now."

Adam Spencer fought for calm. What was wrong with this woman? Why would she argue when he was trying to save her life? Actually, why was he even trying to save her life when he'd had her under surveillance for the past two weeks and suspected she was married to the man who'd killed his wife? The woman who'd meant everything to him.

"Fine." Adam hooked her elbow, started to move toward the doorway. "Walk and talk."

"I will not." She shook him off and stepped back. A spark of indignation flared in her eyes.

Adam was not about to have this conversation right here and now. There was a growing crowd of doctors and nurses moving in to take over the gunman's care and an increasing throng of lookie-loos jockeying for a better vantage point, any of whom might have a camera. And once Maya's picture was plastered all over social media and news outlets, there'd be no saving her, or himself. "Look, Ms. Barlowe—"

One of the firefighters stood and pinned Adam with a curious, not quite threatening stare. "Problem, Jaelyn?"

*Jaelyn?*

"No, I'm fine, Pat, thank you." She narrowed her eyes

at Adam. "I think you might have me confused with someone else."

How could that be? She looked exactly like Maya Barlowe, enough resemblance for them to be twi...uh... oh, no. If this woman was not Maya Barlowe, she might be in even more danger. Not only was she clueless about what was going on, but she'd be considered expendable. He needed time to think, had to figure out what was going on and make a plan to keep both of these women safe. "Um, look, Jaelyn, is it?"

She nodded.

"Okay, listen, I don't expect you to trust me." He dug into his pocket for his ID and a business card, then held them both out to her. "My name is Adam Spencer. I'm a defense attorney from New York City. Please, I can't explain everything right here and now, but everyone in this hospital is in danger as long as you're here."

Her gaze lifted from his credentials. "Me? Why would anyone be in danger from me?"

A second firefighter joined the first. "What's going on, Jaelyn? This guy giving you a hard time?"

"I'm all right, Jack, thank you."

Adam swiped a hand over his scruffy five-o'clock shadow. He needed a shave, and a shower. Neither of which was going to happen any time soon unless he could convince this woman to trust him. He'd obviously come on a little too heavy handed, mistaking her for Maya and figuring she'd jump at the opportunity to escape. That mistake had already cost too much time, and now he had to deal not only with Jaelyn but her two guard dogs as well. "Okay, look, is there somewhere quiet we can talk?"

Jaelyn eyed him for another minute then nodded and handed back his ID. "Follow me."

As she started forward, her apparently self-appointed bodyguards flanked her, leaving Adam to follow behind. Great. This was a disaster. A dull throb began at his temples. As he followed them down the hallway, eyes ricocheting around at the carnage—most of it upended equipment and discarded items people had dropped and knocked over in their haste to flee the gunfire—he caught sight of his reflection in a cubicle window.

Yikes, between the rumpled suit, hair sticking up in every direction, four-day-old scruff, and hardened expression, it was no wonder the woman didn't trust him. He wouldn't have gone anywhere with him either. He reached up and smoothed his hair, not out of any great sense of vanity, but because he needed to come across as a professional, someone these people could trust, or they were all going to end up dead.

When Jaelyn entered a cubicle followed by Pat, Jack gestured for Adam to enter then yanked the curtain closed behind him and stood in front of it, scrolling through something on his phone.

Jaelyn leaned back against the counter, folded her arms across her chest, and gave him her undivided attention. The full intensity in her brilliant blue eyes hit him like a sucker punch. In all the time he'd been tailing Maya, he'd never noticed the incredible power her gaze held. Could it be the two didn't share that quality, despite the eerily similar features and build?

"You have five minutes," she said, "less if they need this cubicle or call for help. Thankfully, there don't seem to be many injuries, thanks to your intervention, or I wouldn't even be giving you that long."

He nodded, appreciating her position, even if he didn't like it. Ignoring the other two men, Adam focused solely on Jaelyn. She was the one he needed to convince, and quickly. "Okay, as I said, my name is Adam Spencer, and I'm a defense attorney. I recently lost a client to a hitman known only as the Hunter. During the attack, he tried to kill me as well, but he failed and I escaped."

Barely. Adam had never come so close to death. He'd practically felt the rush of air as the bullet whizzed past his ear as he'd turned to help his client, just in time to avoid certain death. And he was grateful every day for that instinct to turn to help, though he still lived with the guilt of having failed to save the man who'd trusted him.

"The police can't find this hitman," he continued, "the FBI can't find him, and a host of foreign agencies can't find him. No one can identify him, except for one person, my client who was killed a month ago." Adam believed that the reclusive assassin owned Hack Hunters, a multi-million-dollar cybersecurity company—if only he could prove it.

Jaelyn frowned. "So, what does my sister have to do with this?"

He shifted, uncomfortable beneath her stare, and glanced at Pat, watching them closely, and Jack, still hunched over his phone. How much to tell her? Certainly not of the senator's involvement, not in a curtained-off cubicle in the middle of a chaotic emergency department where anyone could overhear. No, for now he'd just go with the basics. "I believe I know who the Hunter is, and who hired him."

She lifted a brow. "Your client didn't tell you?"

"No, he didn't. Just that he knew the Hunter's identity and that he wanted to turn evidence—"

"In exchange for information." Jack held out his phone to Jaelyn. "Your client was going on trial and was willing to testify to what he knew in exchange for immunity from prosecution."

"Yes." Adam's stomach sank. He'd wanted to share the details with Jaelyn himself, wanted to soften the fact that his client stood to gain a whole new life in exchange for the information he was willing to hand over. "But he also maintained his innocence."

Jaelyn looked up from the phone. "Murder charges?"

"Yes," Adam was forced to admit. "But, again, he maintained his innocence."

"And?"

"And I believed him. I think he was framed." After all, Josiah had been accused only recently of a murder that had happened years ago.

She tapped her bottom lip with one short, unpolished nail, a gesture he'd witnessed Maya do on numerous occasions when stressed. Of course, Maya's nails were painted bright red and sharp as daggers. Then again, what would he expect from someone he suspected was married to one of the most notorious hitmen ever known—a man who moved like smoke, one no one knew for sure even existed because he'd never been careless enough to be seen? Now, if Adam could only find a man no one quite believed was anything more than an urban legend and turn him over to authorities before anyone else died.

Jaelyn shook her head, handed the phone back to Jack. "Okay, so I'll ask again, what does this have to do with my sister? And how am I a danger to anyone?"

"I believe your sister's husband, Hunter Barlowe, is the assassin known as the Hunter."

She sucked in a breath, jerked back as if he'd slapped her.

"I've been..." He squirmed, unsure how any of them would react to the fact that he'd had Maya Barlowe under not exactly legal surveillance. "Keeping an eye on your sister for the past few weeks."

She tilted her head but said nothing.

He hesitated, waited to see if she'd balk. When she didn't respond, he continued. "At first, I thought she might be in cahoots with her husband, and I followed her hoping she'd lead me to him, but in all the time I watched her, I never once saw the two of them together. I got the idea I might be able to approach her, convince her to agree to testify against her husband. Then, three days ago, while I was still trying to decide what to do, I trailed her to a bed and breakfast not far from here. I had no clue why she was there, but now, after she was attacked, I believe her husband may have hired someone to eliminate her. While I can't confirm it, I think she decided to run."

"Why would he want to kill his own wife?"

"So she can't identify him."

"Why would she do that?"

"Because my client, the witness who was killed, was your sister's, shall we say, acquaintance." He shook his head. He should have known about Jaelyn, should have realized Maya had family she might turn to. After the research he'd done on her, how could he not have known she had a sister? "I didn't realize Maya might be visiting family, wasn't even aware of the connection between the two of you."

Jaelyn glanced at her friends, then returned her gaze to Adam and spoke quietly. "What is it you want from me?"

"I want to protect you…and Maya, if possible. And I want to find the Hunter and put him away so I can come out of hiding and get my life back, because he won't stop. He doesn't know my client didn't share his identity with me, so he won't give up until I'm dead. And if I'm right, and he's the one who hired someone to kill your sister, he won't give up until she's dead too."

Jaelyn frowned. "If he's a hitman, why hire someone else to kill Maya? Why not do it himself?"

"To distance himself from the crime." Or perhaps it was the senator who'd hired the hitman to go after Maya. But that was a problem for another time. "I'm quite sure he'll have an ironclad alibi for the time Maya was attacked."

Pat stepped forward. "Jack and I were the paramedics who brought Maya Barlowe in. It didn't appear to be a professional hit." He briefly laid a hand on Jaelyn's shoulder, sent her an apologetic look before turning to Adam. "She was severely beaten."

Adam wasn't surprised. "Probably someone trying to find out what she knew, who she'd told, and what she intended to do next."

"Then why leave her alive?"

"Who knows?" Adam shrugged. He didn't have time for the third degree. "Maybe he was interrupted, maybe he needed the okay from a higher up to complete the job. Whatever the case, the gunman obviously got the go-ahead since he showed up here to finish what he started."

"Okay." Jaelyn straightened and leveled a look at Adam. "So what do you propose?"

Adam's mind raced. He had to get Jaelyn out of there before anyone else mistook her for Maya. At the same time, he had to protect Maya. An idea started to form. "I've done extensive research on Maya Barlowe, had to before I could consider approaching her as a witness, and yet I didn't know about you…"

He let the sentence hang, hoping she'd offer some answer as to why.

Jaelyn heaved in a breath and let it out slowly. "I didn't know about Maya until about a month ago, when the family app from a DNA test I did last year linked me to her profile."

"Hmm…" He chewed that over. Maybe he could turn that in their favor. "Okay, if you didn't know about Maya, there's a chance she didn't know about you. Maybe she just found out as well. If that's the case, whoever's after her may not know about you either. If you'll agree to come with me for now…"

She stiffened.

He plowed on. "I can protect you, and maybe we could keep Maya's identity a secret for the moment. Does anyone else know who she is?"

Pat shook his head. "I honestly thought it was Jaelyn when we brought her in. Then, when Jaelyn walked into the cubicle, I grabbed Maya's purse and we checked the ID."

"As a matter of fact," Jaelyn added, "when Pat came in with her, he yelled that it was Jaelyn Reed. That's what drew my attention in the first place, so maybe…"

"If we let her identity remain a secret, let everyone think it's Jaelyn Reed who was injured, and get you out of here, just maybe I can find the Hunter and keep both of you safe."

"You think Jaelyn's in danger?" Pat asked.

"Even if they don't mistake her for Maya and take her out, once her husband or his employer figure out Maya has a sister, they're going to want to know how much Maya shared with her." But if Adam's suspicions turned out to be true, why had the Hunter's employer allowed Jaelyn to live this long at all? Unless he knew she had no knowledge of her paternity.

Jaelyn shivered.

"How do we keep that from happening?" Jack asked.

Adam shrugged. "I find the killer and turn him over to the authorities."

Jaelyn lifted a brow. "And how do you propose we do that?"

He hadn't said anything about *we*, but he decided to let that go for now. Better to get her to cooperate first, then let her know she wasn't getting involved any deeper in this mess than necessary. "Well, since my best lead is laid up under an assumed identity and unable to answer questions—"

"Stop." Jaelyn held up a hand, then sighed. "If we're going to let everyone believe Maya is Jaelyn Reed, and we look enough alike that even my good friends mistook her for me, why not have me take her place as well. At least long enough to see what, if anything, she left behind in her room?"

# TWO

After overruling Pat's and Jack's objections and ignoring Adam's protests, Jaelyn checked her phone but found no messages from Maya. She quickly changed into street clothes while the three men stood guard outside the locker room. With a headache starting to pound behind her eyes, she yanked the band out of her ponytail, shook her hair free, and massaged her temples.

Not wanting to waste a minute, Jaelyn grabbed her bag and slung it over her shoulder, then pointedly ignored her reflection in the mirror. Who knew? Meeting her own gaze might be just what she needed to force her to reexamine this half-baked plan and change her mind about risking her life to possibly save a sister she barely knew and a man who'd barreled his way into her world uninvited.

Of course, he'd already saved her life, so there was that.

Before she could back out, she pulled the door open and stepped into the hallway.

Pat moved into her path, pitched his voice low. "Are you sure you want to do this, Jaelyn? You don't have to go with him to the B&B."

She nodded, trying to project a confidence she most definitely did not feel. "I'm sure. I'll be fine."

He turned on Adam, patted his shoulder once before tightening his grip. His tone, while still hushed, turned forceful. "You keep her safe."

To his credit, Adam maintained eye contact without appearing at all aggressive. "I will. You guys just take care of Maya and let me worry about the rest."

Jack leaned toward her. "We've already contacted Gabe, and he's on his way. You make sure to keep in touch."

Jaelyn nodded, appreciating all their help. The fact that they'd discuss the situation with Gabe, a police officer who also happened to be a close friend, made her feel somewhat better. But they couldn't wait around right now. They had to get to Maya's room before anyone else did. "Tell Gabe I'll reach out once we leave the B&B."

"Here. I grabbed this when they took Maya to X-ray." Jack handed her Maya's purse and stepped back to let them pass.

"Thank you. For everything." She stuffed the purse into her oversize bag and turned her attention to Adam. "You're sure we shouldn't wait and talk to the police first, right?"

He hooked her elbow and started down the hallway toward the exit. "Right now, they may not have Maya's identity. They most likely went with Pat's assertion it was you, and since the paramedics had her bag, they won't have found her ID yet."

"Once Pat and Jack talk to Gabe, that cat will be out of the bag."

"Yup, that's why we need to get into her room as quickly as possible." He kept his head on a constant swivel as he rounded a corner, then guided her back against the wall. "It would probably be best if no one recognizes you leaving and draws attention to the fact that Jaelyn Reed is fine and well."

She couldn't argue that.

Adam reached behind her, caging her between his arms, then lifted her raincoat hood over her head. He took her hand in his, the strength of his grip the only outward sign of his stress, and started through the emergency department. "Stay close to me."

She wouldn't dream of straying so much as an inch from his side. Jaelyn was no stranger to danger—as a firefighter, her life was potentially in danger with every call—but having someone taking shots at you in a crowded emergency room with no care for any innocent bystanders was something else entirely. She kept her head low, face averted beneath the loose-fitting hood.

As they hurried through the beehive of activity, staff rushed to care for and reassure frightened patients that the threat was over, police officers hammered witnesses with questions as they tried to ascertain what exactly had happened, and people assessed damage and tried to restore order. The gunman had already been moved, no doubt into one of the curtained-off cubicles. While there was broken glass, equipment damaged beyond repair, even a cubicle curtain shredded by gunfire, some semblance of order had begun to return. Carts, trays, papers, and a myriad of other equipment had been picked up and returned to their proper places, and the rushed but smooth flow of activity had begun to reemerge.

As she and Adam hit the doors and stepped out into the cold air, she pulled her hood further over her face.

Lightning flashed, followed almost immediately by a long, low rumble of thunder. Rain beat a steady rhythm as the scent of ozone from the passing nor'easter filled the air. Multi-colored lights from the string of Christmas bulbs hung over the ER entrance reflected from puddles on the ground, and she and Adam splashed across the sidewalk and stepped into the road heading toward the parking lot.

A car fishtailed around the corner of the building, its speed way too fast for the current conditions. And it appeared to accelerate as it barreled toward them.

Jaelyn paused, watching in horror as the vehicle closed in. "Adam    "

"Go!" He shoved her out of the way, then jumped as the SUV struck him and he landed on its hood.

Jaelyn stumbled, fell to one knee on the wet pavement, then regained her footing and whirled back toward him. Run or fight? She couldn't leave Adam hurt.

He saved her having to make the decision when he continued a smooth roll over the roof and tumbled gracefully off the back, then hit the ground running. "Run!"

She turned and fled, didn't look back at the screech of brakes, the slamming of doors, the shouts to stop.

Adam easily overtook her, his stride much longer than hers, and grabbed her wrist. "Go. Left."

She did as instructed, trying to keep a row of cars between her and their pursuers. Stealth wasn't an option as their footsteps pounded against the blacktop, splashing water all the way up to her knees. Jaelyn was a decent runner, tried to hit the track most mornings, but she was nowhere near as fast as Adam. The man could move. For some reason, she wouldn't have expected the lawyer to have such physical prowess.

Adam fumbled a key fob out of his pocket, chanced one quick glance over his shoulder as he hit the button to unlock a dark colored sedan and huffed, "Get in."

She grabbed the handle on the run, used her momentum to yank the door open and swing inside. Her hands trembled as she shoved the seatbelt buckle into the slot, grabbed the chicken stick, and braced herself.

Adam slammed the gear shift into reverse and swung out of the parking spot.

Their pursuers had given up the foot chase and were running back toward their own vehicle.

"Hold on." With barely a glance in each direction for oncoming traffic, Adam yanked the wheel hard to the right as he accelerated out of the lot. The back of the car fishtailed on the slick surface. He battled the wheel to regain control.

Jaelyn's stomach gave one hard roll. A quick glance in the side-view mirror had her heart rate ratcheting up. "They're following."

Barely slowing for a red light, Adam rocketed through the intersection. The car bottomed out, knocking Jaelyn's teeth together, as he hit a pothole. The narrow residential road was not made for the speed at which they were moving.

Adam checked the rearview mirror. "I don't know the area. Is there somewhere I can lose them?"

The SUV was gaining on them, too close to shake. They weren't going to get away without a confrontation.

"Keep your head low." Adam drove with one eye on the road ahead of him and one on the mirror.

Sliding down in the seat, Jaelyn squeezed her eyes closed, shutting out everything around her as she pulled up an imaginary map in her head. They'd left the hospital from the front entrance, the opposite way she'd usually go to head home or to the firehouse. If they could... She jerked up. "Up ahead. About a mile, you can turn onto a dirt fire road."

A glance in the side-view mirror had Adam mumbling under his breath. "Where does it lead? Will we be trapped in there if they follow?"

She braced for impact as the headlights behind them moved closer. "No. There's a network of fire roads throughout the pine barrens. If they're still passable with the heavy rain, we should be able to lose them."

And if they were already flooded, his sedan didn't stand a chance against the SUV on their tail.

Adam slowed.

"What are you doing?" She wedged her feet against the floorboards, then tried to relax so her legs wouldn't break if they hit something.

"Just hold on."

The SUV barreled up on them, moved into the oncoming lane, tried to pull up alongside them on the driver's side.

Jaelyn held her breath and prayed no innocent civilian would round a curve and plow head-on into the vehicle.

The back window on the driver's side shattered. Gunfire?

Adam held the wheel steady, jaw clenched tight. As the SUV jockeyed for a better position, he yanked the wheel hard to the left.

The impact jolted through her.

He pulled the wheel back, sending the car into a dangerous swerve, then recovered enough to hit them again.

Losing its traction on the slippery pavement, the SUV spun out and crashed into a tree.

Adam hit the gas. "Where to?"

They'd already passed the first fire road, so Jaelyn recalculated, pointed ahead of them and to the right. "Turn."

He slammed the brakes, skidded, and she was pretty sure took the corner on two wheels. He slowed and checked behind them as he entered the development.

"Head straight through. You can access the fire roads out the back."

He nodded, breath coming in harsh gasps.

"Are you okay?"

He nodded again, slowed as they bounced over a low berm and onto the narrow dirt path through the woods. Pine trees swallowed them up as the road curved. Thick mud shot from beneath the tires, splattered the windows, splashed in through the broken glass.

"So…" Jaelyn slumped against the seat back, working to steady her nerves. Her hand shook as she tucked her hair behind her ear. "Those were some fancy moves back there."

"Thanks." His grin shot straight to her heart, but his expression sobered much too quickly. "Are you hurt?"

"No, no." She sucked in a deep breath, filled her lungs to capacity for the first time since leaving the hospital. "I'm fine. Are you?"

"I'll be fine."

That caught her attention. "You're injured?"

"Not badly."

She shifted in her seat, reached for the interior light, but he lay a hand over hers.

"No light. It's difficult enough to see with this rain."

Rain pounded against the windshield, the wipers barely clearing it, reducing visibility to just about nothing. "There's a gym bag on the floor behind my seat. Can you grab a towel from it?"

She eyed him another moment, just a quick assessment to be sure he seemed coherent and alert, then unbuckled her seatbelt and shifted to unzip the bag. The towel was right on top, and she yanked it out and handed it to him.

"Thanks." He dabbed absently at the left side of his head, gaze firmly locked on the narrow path through the woods, then tossed the towel onto the back seat.

Even with the interior lights off, the dark contrast of blood stood out against the white towel.

Adam used his sleeve to wipe the blood trickling into his eye again. It seemed to have slowed, but the last thing he needed while trying to drive in this weather was anything impeding his vision. The scrape of metal against a tree had him wincing. "How long until we can get out of here?"

Brow furrowed, Jaelyn shook her head. "I'm not sure. It's difficult to tell where we are."

Thick, black storm clouds dumped gallons of rain in sheets over the windshield despite a valiant effort by the wipers to keep it clear. The car bounced in a hole, stuck for a moment as the tires spun and kicked up a wave of mud, then caught and surged forward. "If we're going to try to get into Maya's room, we need to get there before whoever's after her, and us, does. And before the police."

Jaelyn only nodded and chewed on her lower lip. Leaning closer to the windshield, she squinted, then pointed. "There. See that boulder? My friends and I used to hang out there when we were kids. Okay, I know where we are. Just keep going straight for about a mile. After that, you're going to come into a clearing. Follow the road around the field and you'll come out on a back road we can take to the bed and breakfast."

"Okay, good. That's good." Although he'd have liked to get there more quickly, he didn't dare risk increasing his speed. The rain worked against him, distorting his surroundings until the thick stand of trees all blurred together, making it difficult to navigate the narrow, rutted trail.

Jaelyn sat back, took a few deep breaths.

Adam rolled his shoulders, tilted his head back and forth to stretch his neck and ease some of the tension coiled there. He risked a quick peek at Jaelyn, and in that brief moment, he noticed a problem. "You're sure you're okay?"

"I am, thank you." She lay her head against the seat, and her eyes fluttered closed.

Adam allowed her a few moments of peace to collect herself. Unfortunately, they couldn't afford any more than that. He cleared his throat to get her attention.

When she turned her head toward him without lifting it from the headrest, he debated keeping his mouth shut. Then again, keeping his mouth shut just didn't suit him. "Listen, we might have a problem."

"Really?" She lifted a brow. "Only one?"

He couldn't help but grin. "Well, one more pressing than the others."

"Okay, I'll bite, what's the problem?"

"I don't know if you noticed your sister's clothing when she was brought in."

She frowned. "I didn't. Why?"

"Well…" He gestured toward the well-worn jeans and pink sweatshirt she wore beneath her raincoat. "Maya tended to dress a little more sophisticated."

"Yeah?" She looked down at her clothing. "Hmm."

"We might be able to…alter your appearance enough for you to pass as Maya at the B&B. If, that is, no one there knows her or you too well and you don't stop to chat." And if no one had the B&B under surveillance, because one look was all it would take for someone who knew Maya well to know something was off. He could only hope that the B&B staff didn't know Jaelyn, or they'd have wondered why a woman identical to her had checked in under a different name days ago.

"If you're going to try to pass yourself off as her any-where else, we're going to have to do something about your wardrobe."

Jaelyn started to say something, then caught herself and just waved him off. "One problem at a time, and my fashion choices are not a top priority at the moment."

While he begged to differ, he let the subject drop for the moment. He glanced again at Jaelyn and was surprised to realize he found her more attractive in the faded jeans and sweatshirt beneath her open raincoat than he had Maya with her elegant dresses, pantsuits, and strappy heels. There was something fresh about Jaelyn, an innocence Maya didn't possess. Odd, con-sidering how much alike they looked. He shook off the thoughts. What did it matter to him how the two dressed? It didn't.

And Jaelyn could never matter to him in any other way than providing her protection, not after Alessan-dra's murder. His world had revolved around his wife, and it was his own fault he'd lost her. He tried to shake off the grief, the guilt. They'd do him no good now. There would be plenty of time after her killers were brought to justice to second-guess every decision he'd made that had led to her death. And he had no doubt there was more than one. The Hunter may have pulled the trigger, but Senator Mark Lowell had aimed the weapon.

"Turn up here."

He did as instructed and breathed a sigh of relief when he recognized the gas station on the corner. Only about five minutes to the B&B. "If you roll up your jeans and tighten the raincoat over them, no one should notice."

She shifted to face him. "You really think the way I'm dressed is that important?"

He shrugged, uncomfortable beneath her direct stare. "Look, I'm not the biggest fan of this idea to begin with, which is no secret."

"Nope, you certainly objected strongly enough." She scowled.

He bit back a grin. He had a feeling she might not fully appreciate it at the moment. "But if you're dead set on going through with it, we need to make you as safe as possible."

"What's to say letting people mistake me for Maya is the safest option, considering how she ended up?"

*Touché.* He couldn't imagine what was going on in her mind. She had to be terrified, having a sister she'd never known existed until recently push into her life in such a violent way, getting shot at when she was mistaken for that sister. Though, Adam had to wonder if the gunman had actually meant to kill Maya or if he was hoping to get rid of those protecting her and snatch her. Either way, he had to give Jaelyn credit. All in all, she was holding up quite well under the circumstances.

Jaelyn turned toward him, swiped a tear that had managed to tip over her thick lashes and roll down her cheek.

While he admired her strength, her sensitivity balanced the scales in a way that made her seem fragile. And yet, he couldn't let the overwhelming instinct to protect her get in the way of finding Alessandra's killer.

He wouldn't. Even five years after her death, Alessandra was still his main focus.

"What's she like?" Jaelyn asked softly.

*Alessandra?* She was beautiful, inside and out. Always so quick to put others ahead of herself. She'd have made a wonderful—

"Adam?"

"Huh? What?"

"Maya? What's she like?"

Oh. He didn't know Maya well, had never actually met her, but he'd been watching her for three weeks, had booked the room down the hall from hers at the bed and breakfast so he could keep her under surveillance, but he'd been careful not to come face-to-face with her. He was, after all, Josiah Cameron's attorney, and she certainly knew Josiah well enough, considering she'd been having an affair with him for the better part of a year. Just because Adam hadn't met Maya didn't mean she wouldn't recognize him.

"She's beautiful, of course." His cheeks burned at the implication, and he hurried past the awkward moment. "And smart. Charming. And extremely powerful."

That seemed to catch Jaelyn off guard. "Powerful?"

"She's the CEO of a multi-million-dollar cybersecurity firm."

Jaelyn huffed out a breath. "Seriously?"

"Yes, the firm technically belongs to her husband, but she's the sitting CEO as he tends to other business interests." In most Manhattan circles, the billionaire businessman Hunter Barlowe was thought of as reclusive, eccentric even. He was never seen in public, and his wife kept up appearances. But, if Josiah's information was correct, which Adam had no reason to doubt, Hunter Barlowe's seclusion had more to do with his second, more lucrative career.

"Wow." Shaking her head, Jaelyn lowered her gaze to her hands resting in her lap. "I don't know what to say. It's weird enough trying to wrap my head around the fact that I have a sister…"

Unfortunately, she was going to have to come to terms with a lot more, but now wasn't the time to bring anything else up. They were pulling up to the bed and breakfast, and there was no time to waste. He hit the turn signal and drove into the small parking lot.

Shrubs ran around the perimeter of the three-story building and its wide wraparound porch, offering a sense of privacy for guests and plenty of shadows to conceal a killer lying in wait, despite the sprinkling of white Christmas lights.

"Let's get this done and get out of here. We can worry about everything else later."

She nodded, swiped her hands over her jean-clad legs. "Do you want me to try to clean that cut up before anyone notices?"

"Don't worry about it." He could deal with it later. "I'll keep my head down. You have Maya's purse?"

She pulled it out of her bag, hesitated only a moment, then opened it and dug through. She drew out a key hanging from a round fob with the number 201 inscribed on it, the same as the one Adam had boasting the number 208.

"Yeah, that's it."

She rolled her pant legs up until they'd be tucked beneath her long jacket. "What about my shoes?"

One glance at the running shoes had him groaning inwardly, but he kept his concern to himself. Nothing they could do about it, in any case, so no point in worrying her. "Don't worry about it. You're just going to go straight through the front door and up the stairs on the right. Hopefully, no one will bother to look down at your shoes."

"Okay." She took a deep breath, let it out slowly. "Let's do this."

*Let's not. Let's go on the run, go into hiding, anything but cross that lot and go into that building.* But there was nowhere to run. And there was nowhere to hide.

She reached for the door handle, but he grabbed her arm to stop her. "We can't go in together. You go straight in. Keep your hood up and your head down. I'll watch until after you get inside, make sure no one is around, then follow."

"Got it." She nodded.

"And when you walk, try to project a bit of arrogance, put a little sway in your hips."

She simply lifted a brow then smiled and patted the hand still holding her arm. "I'll see what I can do about that."

When she hopped out of the car and eased the door quietly shut, he slumped in the seat. He wanted to turn the ignition off, not draw attention to the fact there was someone still in the car, but without the wipers keeping the windshield semi-clear, he wouldn't be able to see anything at all. Then again, neither would any potential attackers.

While Jaelyn crossed the lot gracefully, keeping her posture rigid—he'd never take her for her sister. Adam could only hope her husband, if he was the one who'd ordered the hit, wouldn't come himself. She might be able to fool one of his henchmen, but Maya's husband would know in a heartbeat that she was an imposter. The senator would not be fooled either, but that coward wouldn't have the nerve to come after her himself.

When Jaelyn reached the front door, she paused for a moment. Light spilled onto the porch from the enormous Christmas tree in the front window covered in enough icicle lights to let anyone watching get a good look at her face.

"No, don't turn around," he whispered.

She glanced over her shoulder, revealing enough of her face for someone to make the ID, and he was not amused. Right now, he just wanted to get in and search Maya's room, get an idea what they might be dealing with before going up against any more goons.

He only waited a minute, scanning the entire area as he hurried across the lot and up the porch steps. He pulled the door open and rushed inside, then offered a smile and a wave to the owner who was arranging poinsettias while Christmas music played softly in the background.

She smiled at him. "Good evening, Mr. Justice."

"Ma'am." He nodded and kept going through the empty lobby to the stairway. Okay, so as far as aliases went, it was probably corny, but it was better than checking in under his real name with a killer's sights set on him. And, while the fake ID he'd made wouldn't hold up under the scrutiny of someone who knew what to look for, it had worked just fine with the sweet older woman who'd checked him in.

When he reached the second floor, Adam released the breath he'd been holding and hurried into the hallway. A man's voice had him skidding to a stop before rounding the corner.

"...playing games, Maya. We both know you have nerves of steel. Now quit fumbling the key—get that door open, and get inside."

Adam peered around the corner. A short, stocky man stood with his back to Adam and a firm grip on Jaelyn's arm. The instant she got the door open, he shoved her inside.

# THREE

The door to Maya's room slammed open as Jaelyn's assailant shoved her into the narrow entranceway and followed close on her heels.

She stumbled and braced her hands on the wall to catch herself, then shoved backward with all her strength. Still off balance, she led with her elbow as she swung around and landed a satisfying blow to his jaw.

He went down on one knee, then looked up at her and grinned through his bloodied mouth. "You'll pay for—"

Jaelyn followed through with a hard kick to his chest.

Even as his eyes went wide, he wheezed in a breath and doubled over.

Should she go further into the room and take a chance on the window? No. She might end up trapped. With that in mind, she vaulted over him toward the doorway.

He caught her ankle on her way by, and she belly-flopped onto the floor in the entryway, half in the room and half out.

Her chin smacked hard against the wood floor, and her teeth clacked together, sending a rush of pain through her head. Ignoring it, she rolled onto her back.

The attacker whirled toward her, surged to his feet, and lunged.

Jaelyn lifted both her feet and caught him in the gut as he reached for her, propelling him back into the room.

A flash of movement in her peripheral vision made her falter.

And then Adam was there. He dove over her and went after the guy, plowing a fist hard enough into his face to knock the cocky grin right off it.

Jaelyn rolled and pushed herself up to sit, then froze when the world gave one long slow spin. *Okay. You're okay. Just take a moment, sit still, breathe in and out slowly.*

When everything righted itself, she scooted backward. She had to get up. Adam was still fighting this guy, who she had to assume had a weapon even if he'd chosen not to use it against her. And, while someone clearly wanted something from Maya, Adam was nothing more than a target.

With that thought propelling her forward, she struggled to her feet and staggered into the room.

Adam glanced up from where he was digging through her unconscious attacker's pocket. "Hey, you okay?"

"Yeah." She leaned a shoulder against the wall to keep her rubbery knees from betraying her.

Blood ran down the side of Adam's face and into his eye, trailing into his short tawny hair, disheveled from the fight. Actually, his hair had been disheveled since she'd met him. Maybe he made a habit of running his hands through it. Either way, the fact that he'd saved her life again wasn't lost on her, and it didn't exactly sit well. Sure, she counted on her fellow firefighters to keep her safe, but that was a mutual thing, and she'd known most of them forever. This, counting on a stranger to protect her, made her uncomfortable. Seemed she was going to have to make some time to research the enigmatic Mr. Adam Spencer.

"Hmm…twice in one day, huh?" She swiped a trickle of blood from her chin. "So…what? Do you make a habit of rescuing damsels in distress?"

"Only one damsel, honey." He winked at her.

Jaelyn stood where she was a moment, assuring herself the hitch in her breathing and the gentle roll of her belly were the result of her close encounter with a killer and had nothing to do with Adam's charm or the sparkle of humor in his eyes even in the midst of danger.

Jaelyn's last attempt at a relationship had ended in disaster when her fiancé had betrayed her, turned to another woman for comfort when Jaelyn's parents were killed and she'd withdrawn to grieve. The grief had been unbearable, losing them so suddenly, not having the chance to say any of the things she wished she could say. She'd not had a big family, just her parents and her. But then she'd met Ronnie, and he'd become part of the family. They'd planned to get married, have children. And then, as if losing her parents wasn't bad enough, her dreams had been shattered as well.

She cut the thoughts off ruthlessly. They had no place in her life, and she refused to waste even a moment of her time thinking of him. "Are you okay?"

Adam glanced up and found her assessing his injury. "This? Yeah, fine. This is from earlier, just a graze."

"A graze? From a bullet?"

He shrugged as if it didn't matter and continued to dig through the pockets of the man's jeans. "A bullet, glass, it doesn't matter. I'll bandage it or stitch it when I get time."

The injury didn't appear life threatening. As soon as her legs were steady enough to keep her feet beneath her, she'd take care of the wound. "Who is he?"

"No ID." He shoved at the unconscious guy, clearly frustrated, then grabbed a handgun off the floor. "But I did take this off him."

That was no surprise.

Adam stood, dragged a chair from the corner table to the center of the room. He hooked the gunman beneath the arms and started to haul him up.

Feeling a little stronger, Jaelyn bent on the other side of the man and did the same. "Why put him in the chair?"

Lifting a brow, Adam studied her. "In case he wakes up."

"Oh, right." The sooner they got him where Adam wanted him, the sooner she could tend to Adam's injuries.

Once they had him settled, Adam started searching through the room, then disappeared into the bathroom. He returned carrying a bathrobe belt, two leather belts with decorative buckles, and a long red silk scarf, then went to work securing their prisoner to the chair. When he was done, he grabbed one of the other chairs and slid it out for Jaelyn. "Here, sit. You look a little unsteady."

"Just a bit." She sat, her muscles heavy with fatigue.

He pulled another chair close to hers and flopped onto it, panting heavily from exertion.

At least she hoped it was just exertion. "Do you have any other injuries?"

He shook his head, took a few deep breaths.

Watching him, she leaned back in the chair. Muscles she didn't even know she had screamed in protest. Seemed she must have tensed every last one of them while running and fighting over the past few hours, and they'd knotted up in objection. What she needed was a good, long, hot Epsom salt bath. Her eyelids grew heavy, drifted closed.

The muffled sound of a baby crying intruded, snapping her back to reality and the urgency of the situation. Her eyes shot open, jerking her alert. If the scuffle had woken a baby, it would certainly have woken the parents and possibly other guests as well. And if the fight hadn't, the baby's cries undoubtedly would. They had to get out of there before someone decided to investigate or call the police.

Adam met her gaze, jaw clenched so tightly she wondered how his teeth didn't shatter. "I'm going to try to wake this guy up and get some answers from him. Why don't you look around and see if you can find anything? Then we need to get out of here before any of his buddies show up."

Jaelyn narrowed her eyes at his just a little too innocent look. "By get some answers, you do mean you're going to ask politely and hope he tells you what you want to know, right?"

His answering scowl almost made her laugh. "Yeah,

more or less. I'm not going to torture him or anything, if that's what you're worried about."

She lowered her eyes, not willing to admit the thought had crossed her mind. And suddenly she needed to be anywhere else but that room, anywhere she wouldn't have to squirm beneath Adam's intense scrutiny. She shoved to her feet a little too quickly, battled a moment of lightheadedness, then started to search. Of course, it would be easier if she knew what she was looking for.

She took a quick glance around the room, saddened by the lack of holiday festivity, and wondered fleetingly if Maya was as lonely as Jaelyn. What had she been doing staying alone at a bed and breakfast on Christmas Eve? Did she not have any family to celebrate the holiday with either?

She began in the closet Adam must have left open when searching for the belts. She rifled through the mass of designer outfits Maya had hung so perfectly, running her fingers over the expensive fabric. While their taste in clothes might differ tremendously, the need for organization seemed to be something they shared. She felt through pockets, checked the shoeboxes neatly arranged on the top shelf. Nothing but shoes. How long had Maya intended to stay, anyway? Jaelyn wouldn't pack that amount of clothes for a year. And she didn't own half that number of shoes.

Shifting the clothes aside, she looked in the bottom of the closet. Stuffed in the back corner, lost in shadow, was a briefcase. She yanked it out. Locked. No time to try to open it now. Shoving aside the pang of guilt, telling herself it wasn't stealing since she was taking it to try to protect Maya, she set the briefcase on the perfectly made bed.

The nightstand held only a well-worn Bible, and she took a moment to run her fingers over the gold embossed cover, wondering for a brief moment if Maya shared her faith.

A glance under the bed turned up nothing but a few dust bunnies, so she turned her attention toward the bathroom. When she walked through the short, narrow entryway, a door with a clasp and padlock stood to her right. The baby's cries were louder now, and she assumed the locked door must lead to the next room. Anxiety spurred her to move faster. They were already on borrowed time.

Perfume, makeup, toiletries, all lined neatly or arranged in three drawers. How could any one person need this amount of cosmetics? In the cabinet beneath the sink, she found a first aid kit. She set the kit on the counter and opened it, then breathed a sigh of relief that it was well stocked. When she found a box of ammonia inhalants, she briefly wondered what need Maya had for them, then dismissed the thought. What did it matter as long as she had what she needed? Ignoring the niggle of concern, she carried everything out to the bedroom and held a capsule out to Adam, who'd so far had no success rousing their victim. "Here, try this."

"Thanks." He held the capsule under the man's nose.

The man's head snapped back. He shook it as if to clear the cobwebs, then immediately struggled against his bonds. For a brief moment, Jaelyn thought he'd succeed in breaking free, then he stilled.

Adam stood back, carefully out of range if the guy should manage to escape. "All right, buddy, time to have a chat."

The attacker spit at him.

Jaelyn lay a hand on Adam's arm. "Why don't we just go?"

He shook her off. "Did you get what you needed?"

She gestured toward the bed where the briefcase sat. "That's it, and I didn't find the key to open it."

"Maybe it's in *your* purse." Adam held her gaze rigidly with his own.

Jaelyn hadn't thought of that, had already forgotten she was supposed to be Maya. Apparently, it was going to take time for her to get used to this whole cloak-and-dagger thing. Hopefully, she'd master it before she got one of them hurt...or worse.

The attacker studied her, frowned. "You know you can't escape, right... *Maya?*"

Uh oh. Had she just blown her cover?

Adam turned his attention back to the gunman, pointing the man's weapon at him. "Who hired you?"

The man grinned, baring a broken front tooth.

Adam's grip tightened on the weapon, and for a moment, Jaelyn thought he'd fire.

"Look, guy, all I want to know is who hired you. After that, you can go."

Something flickered in the man's eyes. Hope maybe? Then his expression hardened, and he tipped his chair onto the back two legs.

"Fine." Adam took out his cell phone. "If you won't talk to me, you can talk to the police."

Hands bound, the guy simply shrugged.

Jaelyn held her breath, her attention riveted on Adam. "We should get out of here."

He continued to stare the man down. His hands began to shake.

She took the phone from his hand, dialed Pat's number, then walked into the bathroom—where she hoped the gunman wouldn't be able to overhear her—to tell him what had happened and find out if he'd spoken to Gabe.

"Jaelyn, you okay?" Pat asked the instant he picked up.

"I am, yeah. But we need a place to lay low for a little while, regroup."

"I guess you didn't find anything in Maya's room?"

"I wouldn't say that." And she told him about the gunman, careful not to refer to Maya just in case. "I don't think we should wait around for the police, so I thought maybe you could get ahold of Gabe and get them out here while we take off."

"Sure thing. Remember when Jack and Ava were having those problems, and Missy needed to be kept safe?"

Jaelyn remembered well, had taken a few shifts as bodyguard herself at the small house by the beach in Montauk. "Yeah."

"Head out that way, and I'll set the rental up in my name and have the agent leave a key under the mat for you after I talk to Gabe."

"You think she'll do it tonight?"

"Yeah, she's a friend. She'll do it. It won't be freshly

stocked or anything, but she'll run over and leave the key for me."

A wave of relief washed over her, threatening to drop her where she stood. "Thanks, Pat."

"Sure thing. By the time you get out there, it should be done."

She disconnected, rubbed her eyes, and turned to find Adam standing in the doorway.

"Well?"

"Time to go." She hung up and held the phone out to Adam, then held her breath and waited to see if he'd go along with her plan. When she'd finished filling him in, silence descended as they stood staring at one another. "The police are on their way. We should go before they get here."

Still, he remained motionless. Then he frowned, tilted his head, and glanced toward the locked door. "Did you check in there?"

Confused by the sudden change, Jaelyn shook her head. "There's a clasp and padlock. I assumed it was a connecting door to the next room."

Adam's scowl deepened, and he studied the clasp and lock, then muttered, "This is new."

Her heart thundered in her chest, drowning out whatever he said as he bolted into the bathroom and began to rummage through drawers.

He returned bending a bobby pin, then went to work on the lock. "In my room, which is the exact mirror of this one, this is a closet."

Jaelyn leaned closer on tiptoes, held her breath.

When the lock popped open a moment later and he

eased the door open, the baby's cries echoed through the room. On the floor of the closet, secured in an infant seat, a baby stared up at them, tears shimmering in its eyes, streaming down tiny cheeks red and raw from crying.

"No way." Rage poured through Jaelyn as she muscled her way past Adam to reach the infant.

She needn't have bothered, though, as Adam staggered back out of her way, pale as the white blanket tucked around the child.

Even as she unbuckled the seat and lifted the baby into her arms, she whirled on him.

His mouth hung open, his gaze unfocused.

"I thought you said you were watching her?"

"I didn't know." He shook his head, then seemed to come to his senses, and his expression turned to granite. He looked over his shoulder toward the man they'd secured. "Later. Is the baby okay?"

The infant's sobs had lessened upon being lifted out of the seat. The little mouth opened as the baby turned into her. "She needs a bottle, and I have to do an exam."

"Yes, but not here. As long as there's no immediate danger, we have to get out of here. Now." He bent and grabbed the infant seat and the diaper bag lying on the floor next to it. He dropped the seat on the bed. "Secure the baby, and let's go."

She bristled at the order, but he was right. They weren't safe there. They had to get to safety, do a thorough exam, and notify the police.

While Jaelyn cooed gently and resecured the infant in the seat, Adam took one last look around the room, grabbed a pair of leggings and a sweatshirt that were folded on a chair and stuffed them into the diaper bag. At least she'd have something clean to put on if they ever got out of this mess.

Jaelyn shoved the briefcase at him, praying it contained something that would help them, tucked the first aid kit beneath her arm and grabbed the baby's seat. "You ready to—"

"Shh…" He held up a finger, cocking his head to the side, and inched closer to the door.

And Jaelyn heard what had caused him to go on alert—muffled footsteps in the hallway, followed by the hushed sound of men's voices.

Adam bolted for the window, caught their captive's smirk and ripped the heavy drapes apart. He flung the window open, dropped the briefcase into the bushes, and whirled to call to Jaelyn, only to find her at his side. "Drop into the bushes and stay low."

She thrust the baby's seat at him as he turned and aimed the gun at the door.

As soon as she dropped, Adam lowered the baby to her carefully, tucked the gun back into his pocket and followed. He dropped into the thick shrubbery and landed with a splat in the mud.

"Which way?" Jaelyn's voice held a sense of urgency that made it difficult to think.

The baby cried softly. Fearing the cries would give their position away, he had to decide fast.

Try for the parking lot? Or into the dark woods and circle around? Yeah, better to fall back and assess. "Left, go for the woods."

Hunched over the seat to protect the infant as much as possible, she scrambled in that direction before he'd even finished his sentence.

He stayed right on her heels, running in a half crouch, half crawl while twigs and branches caught at his face and mud seeped into his shoes, sucking at his feet with every step. Finding the infant had knocked him off stride, thrown him completely. How could he not have known about the baby? Where had it come from? He'd never seen Maya with a child, not once.

Just before he reached the corner of the house, he heard a door slam open, followed by the gunman he'd held captive screaming they'd gone out the window. He should have put a gag in the guy's mouth, but there was no time to second-guess. "Go, straight across the yard and into the woods."

Jaclyn ran, a full-out sprint despite the slick conditions and the awkward bundle she carried.

A single gunshot startled Adam. He only spared a quick glance back before turning and taking off, the echo hounding him across the neatly manicured lawn and into the thick stand of trees surrounding the B&B. He swallowed the guilt, knowing if he hadn't left their attacker tied up, he might have had a chance to fight back instead of having just been executed. Adam couldn't change that, but he could make sure Jaelyn didn't end up like her sister had, or worse. He would with every breath in his body fight to defend her and this infant.

When he reached the tree line, he crouched beside

Jaelyn, sucked in two deep lungsful of the wet air, then shoved his hair out of his face. "Circle around."

"Do you think we left footprints they can follow?" Jaelyn's teeth chattered as she spoke. Despite the almost knee-length raincoat she wore, her hair was soaked, her feet and legs caked with muck. At least the baby had stopped crying.

He looked back across the lawn. "I doubt it. It's pretty flooded, but it won't be too difficult to guess. We can't flee on foot with an infant, especially in this weather." He gestured toward the thick woods to the right. "It would be shorter to circle around the other way to the lot, so we'll go this way instead."

She nodded, yanked her hood up over her head and followed his instructions. Keeping low, they circled around through the mud and brush. They'd made it about halfway around the building when the first shot rang out and a bullet ricocheted off a tree a foot from Jaelyn's head.

"Get down." He pulled her to the ground and ripped the car key from his pocket then pressed it into her hand. "Belly crawl. Go."

She muttered something he didn't catch but started forward at an awkward crawl over the carpet of pine needles, leaves, twigs, and rocks strewn over the boggy ground, keeping her body between the infant and the gunmen as she dragged the seat along beside her.

Adam slowed, crept forward in a crouch, hopefully drawing their attention long enough for Jaelyn to escape.

A shot rang out, whipped through the bushes far too close for comfort. He went down on one knee, took aim at the first of two figures coming across the lawn toward them at a fast clip, and fired.

The man went down instantly, his partner dove for the ground.

Leaving them to worry if he'd take another shot, he took off, moving as stealthily as possible so as not to alert them to his position. When he reached the far side of the parking lot, he searched for Jaelyn. He had no way of knowing if more men waited for them on this side of the building.

He stood, using a large pine tree for cover, and peeked around the trunk into the lot.

Headlights moved toward him, too fast to be a guest returning. The car fishtailed to a stop in front of him, and Jaelyn swung the door open just before she scrambled over the center console into the back seat.

Adam tossed the briefcase onto the passenger seat as he climbed in, was already accelerating as the door swung shut. "Hold on."

"Go." She turned around to look over her shoulder as he shot out of the lot and onto the road.

With the streetlamps casting enough light for him to see by, he turned off the headlights, navigating the familiar road with little trouble. "Are you hurt?"

"I'm okay. You?" She flopped back into the seat, lay her head back, sucking in greedy gulps of air.

"Yeah." He glanced in the rearview mirror. No one following that he could see.

"Head east toward Montauk."

"All right." Not wanting to stay on the road they'd expect him to follow, Adam made a few random turns, weaving through the neighborhood, then headed for the highway. He lifted the diaper bag over his head as he drove, then dropped it onto the floor behind the passenger seat. "Did Pat say if Maya was doing any better?"

"He said she's still the same."

At least her condition hadn't worsened. "Is the baby okay?"

"I'm checking." She already had the baby out of the seat, examining every inch of its body. Quick glances in the rearview showed her rummaging through the bag and then putting on a fresh diaper. "She's fine. Doesn't appear to be hurt."

Pain threatened to crush him as he slowly released the breath he'd been holding, unsure he could once again live with the guilt of failing to protect a baby as he had his own unb—

"She's okay, Adam." Jaelyn leaned forward, squeezed his shoulder in a gesture of reassurance she could have no idea would mean so much to him, would pull him back from a precipice he couldn't hope to retreat from on his own.

"Good." He nodded, swiped at the tears that had run down his cheeks. "That's good."

The storm had finally let up some, reduced to nothing more than a cold drizzle, as Adam drove toward Montauk. Running wasn't the best idea, but with nowhere to hide and an infant in tow, what choice did they have? Jaelyn's house could be compromised if their pursuers found out about her, and Adam's room at the bed and breakfast was most certainly out of the question. Well, at least he'd had the presence of mind to take his bag when he'd left that morning, so he had all of his belongings with him.

As soon as Jaelyn finished examining the baby, she buckled her back into the car seat then weaved the seatbelt through the back of the car seat to hold it in place as best she could. It wasn't ideal, but it was their safest option.

She hummed softly as she screwed a nipple onto a bottle of formula and fed the baby, rocking her seat gently, soothing her. "It's okay, little one, you're safe now."

*If only that were true.* "I didn't know about the baby, Jaelyn. I would never have left her there if I'd known."

She nodded, staring at him in the rearview mirror. "I know. And I'm not making an accusation, just wondering, how did she get the baby in without you noticing?"

He shook his head. He'd beaten himself up with that question ever since he'd first realized what must be hidden behind that locked door. What if they hadn't found her? He shoved all of the possibilities ruthlessly aside. He didn't have time right now to indulge in what-ifs. The time for that would come later, would intrude at the quiet times, in the dark, in his dreams. A fact he knew all too well from firsthand experience. "How old is the baby? Can you tell?"

"Maybe two months, give or take."

"Okay." The first breath of relief shot from his lungs. "So, if she's Maya's, she had her before I started surveillance. It would have been easy enough to hide her when Maya left her house to come out here, since she packed up the car on gated property, and I couldn't see very well. I tended to follow her whenever she left the property, and I would have tried to get a better view if anyone had visited her, which they didn't."

"What about when you arrived at the B&B?"

He reconstructed the scene in his mind. "I saw her get out of the vehicle, but once I was sure it was her and she was going inside, I circled around, watched for a tail, waited to check in a bit after her so as not to be recognized."

"So, it's possible she could have gotten the baby inside without you knowing."

He nodded, met Jaelyn's gaze in the mirror. "It's possible. I didn't watch her every minute, obviously, or I'd have seen her leave earlier today and she wouldn't have been injured. By the time I heard a woman had been attacked in the woods out here, she was already on her way to the hospital. But we still don't know the infant belongs to Maya."

Jaelyn blew out a breath, ruffling her damp hair, then slumped in the seat and looked down at the child. "No, we don't."

Adam tuned them both out, had to if he was going to be able to think straight. Whatever the situation with the baby, all he could do was keep her and Jaelyn safe. Figuring out who the child belonged to would be up to the police. Unless…maybe there were some kind of documents alluding to the child's identity.

The briefcase they'd taken from Maya's room sat on the passenger seat, calling silently to him while Jaelyn smoothly held the bottle for the baby to drink and rummaged through the well-stocked first aid kit with her free hand.

Jaelyn held a gauze square out to him. "Here, put some pressure on that so it'll at least stop bleeding."

He took the bandage and pressed it against his head, then winced at the sting. "Thanks."

She smiled at him in the rearview mirror, and it tugged at his heart.

"Are you all right?"

"Yes, just a killer headache." She shifted in the seat, groaned. "And maybe a few aches and pains."

Adam grinned. "If I'm being honest, I have to admit to a bit of soreness too. But I'll deny it if you share that with any of your firefighter buddies."

She laughed, the sound filling the warm interior and easing some of his tension. Then she sighed, cuddled closer to the baby. "We're a mess."

He raked a hand through his hair, no doubt making it stick up even worse than it already was. He needed a shower, and about ten hours of sleep, neither of which was going to happen any time soon. "How long does it take to get to Montauk?"

"About an hour, usually." Once the baby finished with her bottle and fell asleep, Jaelyn stuck the briefcase on the floor and scrambled over the center console to the passenger seat. "I secured the seat the best I could for now, since we don't have the base, and covered her with a blanket, but she'll need a better car seat. And we need to cover that shattered window with something."

"I'll take care of the window when we stop. Once we notify the police, we can ask that they bring a car seat when they pick her up."

Something he couldn't read flickered across Jaelyn's

features, then she turned away from him. She flipped down the visor, opened the lighted mirror, and started to clean the cut on her chin. "It'll probably take less than an hour to get there at this time of night with no traffic. When we arrive, I can take care of cleaning that wound for you."

He nodded. Then he remembered she was in pain. "No pain relievers in the first aid kit?"

"Nope."

He hit the turn signal and switched to the right lane. Aside from the gash on her chin, small scrapes and cuts marred Jaelyn's face and hands, and mud covered just about every inch of her. No doubt he looked the same, with the addition of a deep, nasty cut on his temple, one that was most likely full of dirt at the moment. "Will you be okay until we get to Montauk? If there are no pain relievers at the house, I'll run out after I get cleaned up and won't draw so much attention."

"Sounds good, thanks." When she'd finished tending her chin, she flipped the visor back up, dropped back into the seat, and turned her head to study him.

The weight of her stare had him shifting uncomfortably. What did she think of him? The way he'd forced himself into her life? The fact that he was all but stalking her sister? The fact that, despite having been stalking her sister, he'd missed Maya having a child and also missed her leaving the bed and breakfast and being beaten up by someone?

Jaelyn probably viewed him as incompetent at best. In his defense, he rarely made a mistake in the courtroom, but it seemed investigating an elusive hitman while running for your life required a bit of a learning curve. Plus, he was only one man working alone. He couldn't watch Maya twenty-four seven. The thought didn't ease his guilt in the least. As much as he wanted to redeem himself, now wasn't the time. At least, he was trying to convince himself it wasn't.

He inhaled deeply, his breath catching at the instant stab of pain in his ribs. The guy who'd attacked them had managed to land a solid blow, though he didn't think anything was broken. At least, he hoped not. It was probably not a bad idea to take a moment to regroup, figure out where to go next, bring Jaelyn up to speed on the entire situation. And what would she think of him then?

"Penny for your thoughts." Jaelyn's voice jarred him.

"Huh?" He glanced at her, furrowed his brow, stalling since he had no intention of sharing the thoughts coursing through his head just yet.

"You seem...distracted."

"No. I mean, I'm fine." He sighed, relaxed his shoulders, and tilted his head back and forth to ease the tension coiled in his neck. "Sorry. I was just wondering if the police picked up the guy who attacked us yet, got an ID on him."

She took her cell phone out of her jacket pocket, checked her text messages. "Nothing from Gabe or Pat yet."

He studied her expression, then nodded, chewed on the inside of his cheek. Hopefully, whoever was after them bought the Jaelyn as Maya ruse. As long as no one realized Maya was still laid up in the hospital, they would continue to follow him and Jaelyn. If he could just lure them out, he might have a chance of ending this. But was that the best option now that they had an infant in tow? And what if they found out about Jaelyn? He'd do well to keep in mind that Maya might not be expendable—yet—but Jaelyn was. "The guy who attacked us at the B&B…he didn't buy you were Maya."

She lowered her gaze to her hands in her lap.

"If they hadn't shot him—my guess is, for letting us get away—your cover would have been blown. As it stands, we may still have a chance to pull this off."

"Pull what off? I'm not sure what we're even trying to accomplish."

He watched her, her face illuminated each time they passed beneath a streetlamp then plunged into shadow each time they emerged from the puddle of light. He was sorry for her role in this, sorry she'd been dragged from her peaceful life into a dangerous game that might well cost both of them their lives. "At the moment, I'm just trying to keep that baby, you, and myself alive. But the time will come, and soon, that we have to stop playing defense. We're going to have to go on the offense if we're going to put an end to this."

"What *this*?" Her calm, rigid control snapped. She flung her hands out, pinned him with so much anger he figured she probably hated him, and he couldn't even blame her. Especially when he told her what would come next, the only logical step no matter how much he didn't want to take it.

"I know, and you're right. I'm sorry I haven't had time to be more forthcoming about everything."

She stiffened.

What could he tell her? He couldn't divulge any information about the senator's possible involvement yet, considering the man was gearing up for a presidential run and Adam had no actual proof of his involvement. And he didn't dare open up about Alessandra. He couldn't. He barely held himself together sometimes as it was.

"The client I told you about earlier…"

"The one who was supposed to turn over evidence of that assassin you were talking about?"

"The Hunter, yes." If only Josiah had handed over the hit list he'd promised before he was killed. At least he'd have a way to seek justice. "My client said he knew of a hit list and was supposed to turn it over to me the day he was shot."

"You said he never told you who he suspected the killer is?"

"No, he didn't, but I was able to come up with Hunter Barlowe as a suspect based on some of the information he did give me and Hunter's connection to a high-profile client my informant was also associated with. But I still need to find proof."

"And how do you figure you're going to find that evidence?"

Wasn't that the million-dollar question.

"And what does Maya have to do with all of this? You think she knows or suspects her husband is a gun for hire?"

"I believe she may have information about the assassin's identity, although she may not even realize it."

Of course, the fact she'd gone on the run made him believe she knew something, but he refrained from sharing that. Jaelyn could come to that conclusion on her own.

She pursed her lips, studied him for another moment, then turned to look out the passenger window as the three lanes merged down to two. Businesses replaced the woods lining the road. Church bells rang from a beautiful old building, signaling the start of midnight mass. That moved something in him that had been dead for five long years, since the day God had abandoned him and taken Alessandra. He lifted his foot off the gas as they passed.

"I'd like to attend mass." She stared longingly at the building, with its grand steeple, historic architecture, and the lighted Nativity scene out front. "When my parents were alive, we attended mass at midnight every Christmas Eve, a lovely tradition I'm sorry to say I didn't keep up after they passed away."

"You believe in God?" He caught himself too late to keep the words he'd been thinking from popping out of his mouth.

"I do, yes." She looked at him, narrowed her gaze. While he read curiosity in the look, he saw no judgment. "Don't you?"

"I don't know what I believe." This wasn't a conversation he could have right now. "And I'm sorry, but what purpose could you possibly have for going into a crowded church looking like you just went ten rounds in a mud pit with a heavyweight, carrying a child that for all we know was kidnapped, with a pack of killers on your heels?"

She tilted her head, lifted a brow. "Can you think of a better time to pray?"

Well—he huffed out a breath—she had him there. And he could probably have spoken a little less harshly, but this whole mess was getting to him. He gripped the wheel tighter and returned his focus to the road ahead of them.

"I believe God guides us, leads us to where we're supposed to be," she said softly.

He wanted to believe that, had grown up believing it, and then Alessandra had been taken from him, despite every desperate prayer he could utter. "I want to believe in an all-loving God, but I don't understand how some of the atrocities, some of the carnage I've seen, could happen if God influences the minutiae of our lives."

"God isn't responsible for the horrible, unfair things people do to one another, Adam. God teaches us, He guides us, He stands by us, He even forgives us when we mess up royally. At the end of the day, it's our own free will, our own choices, that lead some of us down a darker path. We have to come to God by choice, have to choose to embrace His teachings, choose to allow Him into our lives, into our hearts." She paused a moment. "It's up to us to allow His love to flow through us and touch the people around us. Not everyone makes that choice." She stopped speaking then, and the sense of loss within him increased.

"I'm sorry, Jaelyn. Sorry for all of this."

"It's okay. It's not your fault, and I'm not some delicate person who can't handle stress."

An ironic chuckle escaped before he could stop it. "No, you don't appear to be."

In that moment, the intensity in her gaze, the determination hardening her expression, the strong-willed defiance evident in the lift of her chin and the stiffening of her posture reminded him of Alessandra. His wife had contained the same strength, the same loyalty, the same inner spark that allowed her to embrace whatever life threw at her. And she'd loved him, fiercely, with everything she had, and that loyalty had gotten her and their unborn child killed. Most likely by the same men who hunted him now, though for different reasons.

He'd bumped up against these men before, in another investigation, one that had led him on a five-year mission after the Hunter and the senator had killed his wife to get him to back off. That mission had been brought to an abrupt halt a month ago when Josiah had been killed. "As soon as we get to the safe house, we'll see what the police have to say, and we'll get that briefcase open and see if there's anything in there that will help us."

"Okay." She nodded and turned to look out the window.

And if there wasn't, he had no clue what they'd do next, because these men would not stop until they killed everyone in their way.

# FOUR

As Adam navigated the rutted dirt driveway that led to the small bungalow, Jaelyn tried to recall the layout. Living room in the front, kitchen behind it, short hallway to the right, with a bathroom at the end and a bedroom on either side. Surrounded by woods on three sides with a narrow stretch of ocean behind. The bungalow would provide a secluded, private retreat for them to get themselves together and come up with a plan. Of course, the downside of all that seclusion was that there was only one way in and out by vehicle. If their pursuers somehow managed to find them, they'd be in a tough situation, especially with an infant in tow.

She dismissed the thought as Adam pulled up the circular driveway and stopped beside the cobblestone walkway that led to a wide front porch. They'd just have to cross that bridge if they came to it.

Adam shifted into park and peered through the windshield at the house. "Why don't you go ahead and take the baby in? I'm just going to do a quick perimeter check."

She nodded and reached for the door handle, then

paused. "You don't think they could have found out where we were going, right?"

He shook his head. "No, not yet. But I want to get an idea of what's around us if they do."

"Oh, that's easy…" She shot him a grin as she flung the door open, desperately needing to stretch after going on the run then spending the better part of an hour in the car. "There's pretty much nothing around us."

Not that she blamed him for wanting to make sure. Leaving him to his reconnaissance, Jaelyn unhooked the baby's seat, grabbed the diaper bag, and started up the walkway to the front door. Thankfully, the key was already under the mat, despite the ridiculously early— or late, depending on how you looked at it—hour.

She opened the door to the scent of pine cleaner and flipped on the light. The coastal interior boasted a large, cream-colored sectional. Antique crates served as coffee and end tables, and a massive stone fireplace was bracketed by bookshelves, which were accented with fisherman netting, candles, and seashells. As much as she longed to grab one of the blankets thrown over the overstuffed couch and curl up before a fire, she turned toward the kitchen instead. Relaxing was not an option at the moment.

She hung the diaper bag over the back of a stool and set the infant seat on the floor beside the couch.

The baby sat, brilliant blue eyes wide open, one pudgy fist trying to find her mouth, and seemed to watch Jaelyn.

While she couldn't know for sure the baby belonged to Maya, those eyes were unmistakably theirs. The same ones that looked back at Jaelyn in the mirror each morning. Could this baby really be her niece? Could she truly have gone from having no family to having a sister and a niece in no more than a heartbeat? Her hand shook as she knelt beside the seat and brushed her fingers over the infant's soft, dark hair. "I don't know how this will end, but I'll keep you safe, little one. That's a promise."

"You're right."

Startled by Adam's voice, she jumped to her feet and spun around. Apparently, it hadn't taken him long to check the perimeter and reach the same conclusion she had.

"There is pretty much nothing around."

"Lots of trees, sand and water, but not much else," she agreed.

He set the briefcase and first aid kit on the center island, then stared out the window over the sink at the darkness.

Jaelyn studied the locking mechanism on the briefcase. If she hoped to keep the contents intact, she was going to need a key. Hopefully, Maya kept the key in her purse. She shivered, the cool interior hitting her damp hair and clothes, bringing a chill. But first things first, she needed something warm to drink. She shrugged out of her raincoat and hung it on the back of another stool, then searched the cabinets and came up with hot chocolate and a bag of mini-marshmallows.

At the sight of the cut on Adam's temple caked with mud, she put the briefcase out of her mind in favor of the first aid kit. "I'm making hot chocolate if you want some. Otherwise, there's coffee."

"Hot chocolate sounds perfect. I'm hoping we can get at least a few hours' sleep before we head out."

"Head out where?" She checked the fridge for milk but found it mostly empty. Apparently, the owners stocked the cabinets but didn't keep perishables. She filled the teapot with water and set it on the stove, then turned to find Adam sitting at the counter, frowning down at his clasped hands. "You okay?"

"Huh? Oh, yeah." He scrubbed his hands over his head and stretched his back. "Sorry, a lot on my mind."

That she could sympathize with. "So, you said you wanted to sleep before heading out—where do you plan on going?"

He lifted his hands to the sides, then let them drop back onto the counter. "I have no idea, but the first order of business is to get this briefcase open."

"No." After setting two oversize mugs on the counter and pouring the contents of two hot chocolate pouches into each, she checked on the baby.

She'd fallen asleep, head tilted to the side, mouth open, her soft breaths giving Jaelyn hope she was sleeping peacefully.

Comfortable that the infant was as content as could be under the circumstances, Jaelyn opened the first aid kit. "The first order of business is cleaning that wound before you end up with an infection."

He studied her in that way he had, head tilted, eyes narrowed. It made it seem like he viewed everything with suspicion. Who knew? Maybe he did. But at least he didn't argue as he swiveled the stool to face her.

She moved closer to examine the cut. It had mostly

stopped bleeding, though it would surely reopen when she started cleaning the spattered grime out of it. "This is going to sting a little."

His laughter startled her, lit his eyes—eyes she'd been so sure were brown but now realized held a kaleidoscope of browns and greens highlighted by flecks of gold. Who was this man who'd burst into her life so suddenly, bringing so much chaos and fear? What was she supposed to think of his quiet, somber moods, the way he sometimes lost himself in some thought or another? She knew nothing about Adam…well, except that he was willing to risk his life to save a stranger. She did know that, so she should probably reserve any kind of opinion until she got to know him better. She set to cleaning his wound. "Ready?"

He nodded, and his jaw clenched.

"This could really use a few stitches, but I think I can make do with what I have here. It's going to leave a scar, though." It wouldn't leave the only scar on his face. A small crescent-shaped one curved around the corner of his right eye, and a long, faint, barely noticeable mark ran along his jawline. Between the scars, the agility he'd shown while running, and his fighting skills, she had a feeling Mr. Tall, Tawny, and Brooding didn't spend all of his time sitting behind a desk or defending his clients in a courtroom. "You seem to be in good shape for a lawyer."

He frowned at her for a moment, then laughed out loud. "What? Lawyers aren't supposed to be athletic?"

Heat burned in her cheeks. She didn't even know how she'd let the comment slip out. She must be overtired, something that tended to make her lose her filter. "I didn't mean… I just meant it doesn't seem like you sit behind a desk all day."

The tea kettle's shrill whistle interrupted the awkward moment, and she hurried to grab it before it could wake the baby. Once she'd turned off the burner and filled the mugs, she stirred the drinks and added a generous amount of marshmallows, then brought them both to the counter and set Adam's in front of him.

"Thanks."

"Sure thing." She finished cleaning and bandaging his wound in silence. At least that might keep her from putting her foot in her mouth again. "There you go. Good as new."

"Thank you." He held her gaze. "Listen, there are things we need to talk about, things I need to tell you, but for now, I have no idea how long we might be safe here, so why don't we see what's in this briefcase and then take showers and get some sleep?"

She nodded. Considering the fact she'd just come off a twelve-hour shift before going on the run for her life, she was about ready to fall over. And technically, she was supposed to be back on in six hours. She had a feeling she wasn't going to make her 7:00 a.m. start time. "I'm going to have to call out of work."

Adam glanced at her, frowned. "I'm pretty sure, since everyone thinks you're laid up in a hospital bed, they'll assume you're not coming in."

True. She hadn't thought of that, but it still didn't sit right. She texted Pat, asked him to take care of letting her supervisor know she needed the day off, then pulled

Maya's purse out of her bag and dug through until she found a key ring with four keys. One was obviously a car key, and one was smaller than the rest. The briefcase key? She said a quick prayer as she stuck it into the keyhole and turned, and an equally quick thank-you when the lock released.

Before she had a chance to open the case, her phone dinged with a text. Reluctantly, she shifted the briefcase aside in exchange for her phone. To his credit, Adam didn't immediately dive on the case when she set it aside. She'd be lying to herself if she didn't admit she probably would have if their situations were reversed. She opened the text and frowned.

"Something wrong?"

"Huh?" She glanced up to find Adam's eyes intently focused on her. "Oh, sorry. It's from Pat. He says they found a body tied to a chair in Maya's room. Gabe is freaking out because we left the scene, though Pat says he explained everything to him, and they want to know if we killed him."

"Who's Gabe?"

Jaelyn shook her head. "Gabe, uh, he's a friend… and a cop."

"Which first?" Adam held her gaze.

"It doesn't matter." She typed a quick answer back to Pat.

"Does anyone really think you'd have executed a man who was tied up and not only didn't pose a threat but couldn't even defend himself?"

She glanced up at him. "They know I didn't kill him, but they don't know you at all."

He nodded and lowered his gaze. "Fair enough."

When she checked the baby again, she found those intense infant eyes open and staring at her. It brought an unexpected surge of wonder. If she truly was Maya's, this child was some of the only family Jaelyn had left. She suddenly felt fiercely protective of the girl. She wanted to keep the child close, love her, care for her, protect her…but first she had to make sure that she was actually her niece. "We have to do something about this baby."

He lifted a brow. "Like?"

"Find out who she belongs to, for starters."

He frowned, shook his head, and finally chanced a quick glance toward the seat before averting his gaze. "You don't think she's Maya's?"

"I don't know." Jaelyn started to pace now. "But we can't assume she is. We can't assume anything. We need some things from the store. She's going to need diapers and formula before too much longer, and we need some way to take her footprint so we can send it to Gabe in the hope of identifying her."

"And if she is Maya's and that identification throws up a red flag that puts her in more danger?" He crossed an ankle over his knee, lifted his hands to the sides. The fact that his argument made sense only served to annoy her. "Besides, we're going to have to make do with the supplies that were left in the diaper bag, since there's not much open on Christmas Day."

She opened her mouth to argue with him, then stopped. How could she have forgotten it was Christmas morning? Her mind was frazzled, her nerves shot. She really did need sleep.

"I'll tell you what." He lowered his foot to the floor, leaned forward with his elbows resting on his knees, hands clasped together. "Notify Pat about the baby, have Gabe look into it. As soon as we hear something back from him, we can decide how to handle it. If he doesn't find any missing person reports matching her description by tomorrow, we'll either go the footprint route and try to identify her, or turn her over to social services. In the meantime, we'll go through the documents in the briefcase more carefully and see if we can figure out who she is."

Oh, how she hated the fact that he was right. "If it turns out she's Maya's, do you think I could get emergency custody?"

She wasn't sure why she'd asked that. But she knew what it was like to be alone in the world and didn't want that for this baby.

Adam's gaze shot to hers and the compassion in his eyes anchored her.

"If she doesn't have any other family members to take her in, of course." The fact that she didn't even know if her own sister had family weighed heavily on her.

He nodded slowly, raked a hand through his hair. "Yeah, I could probably do that, under the circumstances. There is one way we may be able to determine if Maya's her mother fairly quickly."

"Oh? And what's that?"

"See if we can get a look at her medical records. Do you know anyone at the hospital who might be able to do that without a court order?"

"Hmm...maybe." Hope surged through Jaelyn. She hadn't realized until that moment how badly she wanted the baby to belong to Maya, not only because the thought of her sister possibly being a kidnapper shot daggers through her, but because if the baby belonged to Maya, Jaelyn might have some hope of remaining a part of her life. Which brought her to the next pressing thing.

Jaelyn pulled the briefcase toward her, then paused. There wouldn't be much time before she needed to tend to the baby again. "Why don't you go ahead and jump in the shower while I feed and change the baby, then I'll take a turn? After that we'll sit and go through the briefcase." She ran her hand over the top of it, wondering what it held but nervous about what they'd find. "I could use a few minutes to gather my wits before we try to make a plan. Because the stakes just got a whole lot higher with the addition of the baby. No matter what we decide to do, her safety has to be the priority."

"That we can agree on." He nodded and stood. "I'll only be a few minutes."

That was fine, because she really needed to have this whole mess behind her, needed to learn the truth about her past so she could move on with her life, and she most definitely needed to put Mr. Adam Spencer behind her before he snuck past her defenses and she allowed him to get any closer.

They took turns showering and he donned a cleanish pair of jeans and a long sleeve pullover he'd hurriedly rolled up and stuffed into his bag that morning. Since Jaelyn had kept the baby with her while she showered, it had saved him having to watch her—however much of a coward it might make him. Even though he'd give his life to protect the baby, he wasn't yet ready to have the responsibility of being left alone to care for her.

He'd already walked the perimeter once more while he waited, and the lack of an exit strategy bothered him. There was literally no way out of the safe house if they were found. And it wasn't like someone would need an army; with one attacker positioned on each side of the house, the only means of escape would be either the narrow driveway or by water, and they couldn't very well swim in the waning storm with the baby in tow.

While there should be no way anyone could know where they'd gone, he couldn't help feeling like a sitting duck. The wall of windows overlooking the expanse of ocean at their backs was a security nightmare. With the exception of the small clearing the house sat amid, they were surrounded by thick woods anyone could sneak through.

Supposedly, not many people knew where they were, but the senator's reach was far and wide. The instant the senator learned of Jaelyn's existence, if he didn't know about her already, he'd have people searching under every rock for even the tiniest tidbit of information on her. He'd know within minutes of her connection to Seaport Fire and Rescue where she was a volunteer firefighter, and soon after he'd know everything there was to know about anyone and everyone even remotely connected to the place. Including where Pat might recently have rented a bungalow at the last minute on the very night one of his goons was killed and Jaelyn disappeared.

And if he did already know about her and had let her live this long, it was only because she was blissfully ignorant of the situation. Once he found out Maya had shown up, that would no longer be the case.

Of course, if they could find the killer and bring him down, escaping would no longer matter.

Jaelyn wandered into the kitchen with the baby, wearing the sweatshirt and leggings he'd grabbed from Maya's room. She gestured toward the briefcase he'd somehow managed to keep from rummaging through without her. "Do you want to go through it in the living room?"

"Sure." He did as she suggested, not caring where it got opened as long as it did.

She curled up in the corner of the couch with the baby in her arms, kissed the top of her head, and Adam sat beside her and set the briefcase on the coffee table.

The way she gazed down at the little girl who'd wrapped one tiny hand around Jaelyn's finger made him wonder if she'd really be willing to give her over to anyone else. She was getting too attached. When Jaelyn simply looked up and grinned at him, it shot straight to his heart. "Let's see what we have here that might help us out of this situation."

Adam shook his head, shifted his gaze downward toward the briefcase to hide the smile he wasn't ready to share. He wasn't kidding when he'd said Jaelyn was something, and she'd piqued his curiosity.

He cut the train of thought off immediately. Just because her self-assured grin touched him at a moment when he was feeling down, just because her matter-of-fact attitude was refreshing, just because she was a beautiful woman who seemed to always put others first, didn't mean he was attracted to her.

His focus needed to be on finding the men who were after them. Besides, Alessandra was the only woman who mattered to him, the only woman who could ever matter.

"You know, I was thinking about something," she said.

Still distracted, he turned to her. "What's that?"

"You said earlier that the police and the FBI and a number of other agencies weren't able to find this guy. Why not?"

"What do you mean?"

"Why can't they find him? If you could figure out who he is, why couldn't they?"

"Because they didn't have Josiah Cameron. If he hadn't come to me, hadn't given me a place to start looking, I wouldn't have any idea who he was either." But once Josiah had told him about the senator's connection, it was easier to follow the dots to Hunter Barlowe. "Josiah worked as an aide for a high-profile senator, one he suspected employed the Hunter to get rid of anyone who stood in his way."

"Stood in the way of what?" She kept her voice low, gently rocking the baby as if it was the most natural thing in the world to her.

"Of getting anything he wanted." And he'd stop at nothing. "Josiah said he had proof, said he could provide a coded hit list that proved the senator had paid for certain murders."

"You suspect my sister's husband is the assassin you're looking for, but how could that be? It's hard to believe a regular guy can just run around killing people and not get caught."

"Hunter Barlowe is far from a regular guy." At least, according to the surprisingly little information Adam had been able to dig up. "He is the reclusive billionaire owner of Hack Hunters, a cybersecurity company. A lot of people think he's so good at security because he's paranoid, keeps to himself because it's safer that way."

"But you don't?"

"I think it's a convenient cover. I think he leaves the day-to-day running of his business to others so he's free to roam the world fulfilling obligations for his real career."

"As an assassin for hire."

"Exactly." He understood it was a lot to process at once and sat back to give her a minute, see if she had any more questions. "And who is there to notice he's missing? No one. The perfect alibi, really."

She chewed on her lower lip for a moment, as if trying to decide whether or not to ask something.

He suspected he knew what she wanted to know, but he'd wait for her to decide if she was ready for the answer.

When she did finally ask, she spoke so quietly he could barely hear her. "Do you think she knew? Maya? Do you think she knows what her husband is, what he does?"

His heart ached to hold her, to ease some of the pain

this was surely causing her. But he couldn't. All he could offer her was the truth. "I think she found out. And when she did, I think she told Josiah. He came to me determined to take down not only the Hunter but his clients as well, at least one of them—the senator."

She nodded as tears tracked down her cheeks.

Adam lay his head against the back of the couch, let his eyes fall closed. He took a few deep breaths. They needed sleep, both of them, if they were going to be able to think clearly, but they needed to go through the briefcase first, see if there was anything to help them, to give him something to think about while he tried to rest after.

When the baby fell asleep, Jaelyn stood and lowered her into the seat then buckled her in. When she returned to her spot on the couch, she shifted the briefcase closer and opened it.

He looked over her shoulder and caught the scent of strawberries from the shampoo she'd used.

She let out a low whistle. "Wow. I've never seen that much cash. How much do you think is in here?"

Adam shifted his attention to the pile of money sitting in the case. He lifted one of the bundles, thumbed through it. "If they're all hundreds, there's got to be at least a hundred thousand in here, probably more."

Jaelyn lifted the cash out and set it on the coffee table beside the case. "Do you think it's real?"

"Oh, it's real all right." But he held one bill up to the light, checked it thoroughly. "Or an amazing counterfeit."

"Why would she have so much cash in a briefcase?"

She picked up a folder, then gasped at the sight of the two handguns lying beneath it.

Adam removed the guns, checked to see if they were both loaded—they were—as Jaelyn opened the folder and leafed through the contents.

"If I had to guess, I'd say she was going on the run. She must know something, must have suspected someone was after her." It would make sense, all things considered. As much as he'd like to spare Jaelyn from learning about Maya's indiscretions before having the chance to meet her and see what kind of person she truly was, he couldn't leave her in the dark. It was too dangerous. "Jaelyn, there's something you should know. About Maya and Josiah."

"They were lovers?"

He nodded. "Yeah. I'm sorry."

"It's not your fault. Besides, I don't judge people based on one action. Whatever Maya's reasons for betraying her marriage vows, she didn't deserve to end up beaten unconscious."

"Has she woken yet?"

"Oh, yeah, sorry. I forgot to tell you, when I texted Pat, he said she hadn't."

"Do they expect her to?"

Instead of answering, she massaged the bridge of her nose between her thumb and forefinger, then tossed the folder she'd been perusing back into the briefcase when the baby gave a demanding cry. So much for sleeping.

She lifted her from the seat, cradled the small bundle against her, and sank back onto the couch. "They expect her to, but who knows. I'm not there, so I don't know the full extent of her injuries. I've been a little busy with everything else."

Adam perched on the edge of the couch so he could face her. "Hey, you okay?"

"I don't even know at this point. There's so much going through my head, and I don't know what to make of any of it." She bounced the baby in what seemed like an automatic gesture, reducing her cries for the moment.

The contents of the briefcase called to him, begged him to search for answers that might point him in the Hunter's direction. He ignored it. "Do you want to talk?"

She shook her head, then stood with the baby, took one of the prepackaged bottles from the diaper bag, and screwed on a disposable nipple. "I wouldn't even know where to start. My entire life was a lie. My parents are gone, so I can't ask them anything. I have no other family. I lost Ronnie, my fiancé, when I couldn't move past my grief. And now…now, I have a sister I never knew about, who may or may not be married to a notorious hitman, who may or may not be trying to kill her. And me. Add in an infant that may or may not belong to said sister, and where does that all leave me?"

Actually, holding up quite well, all things considered. "I'm sorry for all of this, Jaelyn. All I can tell you is I'll do my best to help keep you, Maya, and the baby safe and try to find the answers you're searching for."

"Right now, there's only one question burning a hole in my gut." She laughed, but it held no humor. "I can't imagine why my parents would have given her up, and they're not here to give me the answers I need."

Given her up…? Ah, man. Now what? Should he

keep the information to himself? Let Maya be the one to tell her she was adopted, so it would at least come from family, even if it was family she didn't know? No, he couldn't let her continue on blind. Not only would it hinder her search for answers, it might well prove deadly. "Listen, Jaelyn, I'm sorry to be the one to tell you this, and I wish there was a gentler way to say it, but your parents didn't give Maya up."

She frowned, kissed the baby's dark hair, and gazed down at her. "What do you mean? Was she abducted?"

He shifted to the edge of the cushion, uncomfortable no matter his position. "Maya was adopted when she was an infant, when her birth mother gave her up."

"Her…" She paled. "What?"

"I'm sorry. I didn't know about you, so I don't know why you weren't placed in the same home, but when you're ready, if you want, I can pull some strings and try to find out. The one thing I do know is that your mother was from New York City, lived and worked in Manhattan." That wasn't the full truth. He knew who her biological dad was but didn't dare say…not yet.

Her expressions ranged from pain to grief and every emotion in between as she rocked back and forth with the baby clutched close, crying softly as she sank further into the cushions. "Thank you for being honest with me."

He leaned back, giving her a moment to process what little he'd been able to tell her.

It didn't take her long to pull herself together and return her attention to the briefcase. She took out the folder she'd been looking through and a few others then handed them to him. "These appear to be documents regarding the cybersecurity firm, but I can't make anything from them."

He took the folders, allowing his gaze to linger on her raw cheeks and puffy eyes for a moment. She needed rest. "I'll look through them. Why don't you go ahead and get some sleep?"

"Thank you, Adam, for everything. And don't worry. I'm far from fragile. I might take a few minutes to wallow in the confusion, but I bounce back pretty quick." She stood and set the bottle aside to change the baby's diaper. Once she had the baby settled back in the seat, she returned to the couch, set the seat beside her and absently stroked the baby's hand. Then she gave him a smile.

"Come on. We'll go through the rest of this quickly together then get a little shut-eye and start out fresh in the morning."

Her smile left him with a feeling of relief and admiration, though he was reluctant to dwell on that last one. Instead, he turned his attention to the contents of the briefcase. There had to be something there to help them find answers before their attackers could track them down again.

He leaned forward and shuffled through the folders. The first contained financial information from the business.

"What is it?"

"Bank accounts, copies of stocks and investments, and a flash drive labeled tax returns taped to the inside cover." Without a computer at his disposal, he'd have to accept that's what it really was for now, but he'd confirm at the first opportunity.

He turned the folder over on the coffee table and grabbed the next, which contained lists of names, dates, and account numbers. Clients, maybe? The Hack Hunters logo was at the top of each page in the thick dossier.

Jaelyn frowned. "Why would she have taken off with financial information from her husband's company?"

"Good question." Although, she was the CEO of the company, so it was possible she was working from the road. But he didn't believe that for a second.

"Do you think it's possible she knew you were tailing her?" Jaelyn asked. "Maybe she mistook you for an assassin and fled?"

"Huh. I hadn't thought of that. I tried to be careful, but I suppose it's possible she spotted me."

"Especially if she had reason to believe her husband might be trying to kill her and had already murdered her lover."

Since he couldn't argue with her logic, he paged through the document, skimmed over the names, then backtracked when he recognized the name Mark Lowell. *Well, what do you know. Good ole Senator Lowell just happens to be a client.*

He ran a finger along the lines following his name and let out a low whistle. Seemed the senator had doled out a fortune for cybersecurity. A list of dates, amounts, and letters were detailed beneath the senator's name. Then one date jumped out and gripped him by the throat, threatened to choke off his air supply. He wheezed in a deep breath, his hand shaking as he followed the line of data with his finger. The date—a date from five years earlier, the same date his wife had been killed—was followed by the amount of two million dollars and the letters AS. Her name eased out on the softest whisper. "Alessandra."

The hand he shoved through his hair shook violently. Was he looking at the hit list Josiah had told him about? Was that line the hit on his wife? Coded, Josiah had said. Could it simply have been disguised to look like a Hack Hunters business document? Had Maya found the list? Planned on giving it to Josiah before he was killed?

"Hey." Jaelyn gripped his arm. "You okay?"

He couldn't talk about this right now, was barely keeping it together with all the questions pounding in his head.

Jaclyn lowered her hand, offered a tentative smile. "Well, if that's how you react when someone figures out something you hadn't thought of, this partnership is doomed."

"I'm sorry." He stood abruptly, needing to get out of there. Then he spotted the small tracking device set in the corner of the briefcase. Had Maya place it there in case someone stole the briefcase? Or had the bug led the Hunter's men to Maya at the B&B?

Fear for Jaelyn's and the child's safety had him hoping it was the former. Alessandra was already lost. While he'd do everything in his power to see she had justice, he couldn't sacrifice any lives in the pursuit of that goal. "Sorry. I guess I'm jumpier than I realized."

"Don't worry about it. Believe me, I understand."

*No, you really don't.* "Get the baby's things together. We're leaving."

"Leaving? I thought we were going to get some sleep?"

"Yeah, well, so did I, but plans change." He cringed at the harshness in his own voice, and yet he couldn't help himself. His insides were twisted into knots. Rather than say anything he'd come to regret, he gestured toward the mess of papers on the coffee table. If he returned to them, he'd never be able to walk out. His conscience wouldn't allow it. "Can you put that stuff back together in the briefcase, please?"

She frowned but only said, "Sure."

Leaving her confused and seemingly a bit wary of him, not that he could blame her, Adam headed for the bathroom for a moment alone and to hide the tracking device. If their pursuers thought they were remaining at the house for the night, they might wait until later, when they could be fairly sure everyone was asleep to attack. If he destroyed it, they might come on the run.

Once the door was shut behind him, he purposely unclenched his hands, lay the device on the counter, then rested his hands on either side of it.

He had to get control of himself. Going off half-cocked wasn't going to help anyone, nor would it get Alessandra the justice she deserved. If the papers Maya had secreted in her locked briefcase were what he suspected—not a Hack Hunters client list, but the Hunter's hit list, with names, dates, and amounts all neatly outlined beneath the client who'd ordered the hit—he might finally have the ammunition he needed to take down not only the Hunter but also his clients. If he could stay alive long enough to see it through.

# FIVE

Sitting on the couch, with her feet tucked beneath her and the baby cradled snuggly against her, Jaelyn inhaled deeply the scent of the baby wash she'd used on the infant earlier. She listened to the girl's soft breaths as she slept. Jaelyn probably should have left her sleeping in the seat while Adam was in the bathroom, but since he seemed fully intent on going on the run again, she had no idea how long the little girl would have to be strapped in. Better to keep her close while she could.

She shifted so she could look down at the infant sleeping against her chest. How could Maya have left her alone? What kind of woman would do that? A desperate one. So what had she gotten herself into? Was the baby even hers? Or had she taken her from someone? Was there a desperate mother searching for her child even as Jaelyn sat holding her?

She sighed. That wasn't fair. She had no idea what was going on with Maya. She'd probably done the only thing she could to keep the baby safe from whoever had hurt her. Either way, they had to deal with the situation as soon as Adam returned. Taking the infant with them to keep her from immediate danger was one thing, but keeping her in temporary custody was something else entirely. "I'll take care of you, little one. One way or another, I will keep you safe. That's a promise."

With a renewed sense of determination, Jaelyn scanned the papers Adam had been reading. Finances weren't really her thing, but whatever he'd seen had seemed to upset him. She tried to make sense of the lines, names and random letters. When a headache started to brew behind her eyes, she gave up and stood, careful not to disturb the baby, then stuffed the documents back into the folder. Mr. Bossy had told her to pack everything up so they could get out of there, and while she assumed he had his reasons, she definitely planned on asking him if he ever came out of the bathroom.

She returned the baby to the infant seat and strapped her in, then set the carrier on the floor. She hadn't found any kind of coat in the diaper bag, so she had to settle for tucking the thin knit blanket back around her. Once she had the girl settled, she scooped up the remainder of the folders Adam had set aside, tapped them against the coffee table to align them, and started to put them in the briefcase. Then the name Jaelyn caught her eye, printed neatly with a Sharpie on one of the folder tabs. She stuffed the others into the case, put Maya's purse back into her own bag, and set the briefcase, her bag, and the diaper bag all beside the front door next to Adam's bag. With that done, she was ready to go. She flopped onto the couch with the folder and propped her feet on the coffee table.

And a second later, she lurched upright. What in the world? The folder contained a copy of Jaelyn's birth certificate. Why would Maya have a copy of Jaelyn's birth certificate? Jaelyn had never seen this copy, which listed a birth mother whose name she didn't recognize, issued from a hospital in New York City that she'd never heard of. No father was listed. Her own copy contained the names of the only parents she'd ever known. Even stranger, the folder contained a Montana driver's license in Jaelyn's name—odd, considering she'd never set foot in Montana—and several credit cards in the name Jaelyn Reed.

A niggle of fear crept up Jaelyn's spine, settled at the base of her neck, and began to throb. For some reason, the sister she hadn't known existed until a month ago had a bagful of forged documents in Jaelyn's name. How was that even possible? And for what purpose?

"Ready?"

Jaelyn jerked toward the doorway, putting a hand over her chest. "What are you trying to do?" she asked him. "Save whoever's after us the trouble of killing me by scaring me to death?"

Humor lit his eyes and she noticed they were puffy and red as if he'd been crying. He shrugged.

"Mmm-hmm. Well, for now, sit down for a moment. We have a few things to discuss before we leave here."

When he simply stood staring at her, she acquiesced. "Please."

"We have to get out of here, Jaelyn, and I prefer to do so before we lose the cover of darkness."

His sense of urgency tweaked her radar, especially

since some of the problems she had rattling around in her head seemed more important to her than leaving a place where she felt fairly safe. "What aren't you telling me? We've only been here a few hours. It won't even be light out for another hour or more. Why not get some sleep before we go?"

He seemed to look straight through her then. His expression softened, and she saw a gentler side of him, a side he seemed to keep hidden most of the time. The moment didn't last long before he clenched his jaw. "There was a bug in the briefcase."

She struggled to bring her thoughts back to the conversation. "A bug?"

"A tracking device. I left it in the bathroom so it will remain stationary, as if we're still here. I'm hoping whoever's following the case will figure we've decided to stay put and we can slip out undetected before it gets light."

A range of options flickered through her head in an instant before she reached the same conclusion. They had to go. If he could navigate the long driveway through the woods with the lights off, maybe they could escape unnoticed. She glanced at her watch. Which told her they didn't have much time. She stood and took a last look around to make sure she hadn't forgotten anything.

Adam walked through the house, methodically checking each window, keeping to the side as he glanced out from every imaginable angle. He was so determined to keep them safe, her and the baby. Two strangers.

And something in her changed, opened, allowed

room for both him and the baby to pull out feelings she'd thought long buried. Instead of being comforting, the newfound emotions only confused her. For years, Jaelyn had been able to keep the wall around her heart well-fortified, keep from trusting anyone enough to even consider the temptation of a relationship. No way would she allow this rugged stranger who'd barreled uninvited into her life so aggressively to get to her. No thanks.

He glanced over at her, then paused and frowned. "Is everything okay?"

"What?" She hadn't even realized she stood so still, watching him, tears slipping down her cheeks. She wiped them away. He'd been honest with her so far, from what she could tell. Didn't he deserve the same in return? "I'm sorry. I was just thinking about my parents. And Ronnie."

Giving up on the surveillance for the moment, he walked to her but left some distance between them. She blew out a breath. "When my parents were killed, I was engaged to a man I thought I'd spend the rest of my life with. I had a hard time dealing with their loss." Memories of that time—of the crushing grief—came back to her.

"I couldn't eat, I couldn't sleep, I was…just…sad all the time. And Ronnie, well, I was lonely one evening, needed company, so I knocked on his door. When he didn't answer, I tried the doorknob and it was open. His car was in the driveway, so I walked in, started to call out, when I heard a woman's voice." The pain punched a hole through her once again, and five years melted away in a single heartbeat. "He was cuddled on the couch with his arm around another woman. He told me he was in love with her and asked me to leave. And my heart shattered."

"Ah, Jaelyn. I'm so sorry." He started to reach for her then seemed to think better of the idea and lowered his hand.

She was grateful for that. Her emotions were too raw. She needed the strength to finish telling him without falling apart, and that would be easier without the warmth of his hand enveloping hers.

She swiped at the tears that had begun to fall, anger creeping in to battle some of the sadness. She'd come to terms with Ronnie's betrayal long ago, was glad in a way that she'd found out exactly what he was before she married him. "It's okay. At least, it is now. But since then, I've never taken the risk of needing some one again, learned to rely on myself, on my friends, but I never let anyone get too close."

"I can understand that."

The fact that he'd simply understand without offering advice or launching into a rant about what a terrible person Ronnie was brought a wave of relief. He'd offered exactly what she needed, simple understanding. "Anyway, there's no time for this…"

"I'm glad you were able to trust me enough to talk to me." He did reach for her hand then and led her toward the door when she put her hand in his. "You're right, we do have to go now."

They'd already used up enough time.

She returned her attention to getting out of there and

grabbed the car key. "I'm going to go warm up the car for the baby."

"I'll do it." Adam held out his hand for the key.

"Please, let me…" How could she explain how confused she was, how parts of her warred with each other? She couldn't. At least, not right now. She didn't even know who she was. Why had her parents not simply told her the truth? "I need a moment."

"Okay, sure." He looked out the front windows, then gestured her forward. "I'll grab the bags and follow you out. Just start the car, though, and come right back in for the baby."

"Got it. And Adam…" She paused, waited for him to look at her. "Thank you. For everything."

"You bet."

She lifted her raincoat from the back of the chair and took it out the front door with her without putting it on. When she reached the porch, she shook and wiped as much of the mud off as she could before shrugging into it.

Her thoughts shifted from Ronnie's betrayal to her parents. How could she explain to him how deceived she felt? How painful it was to realize her parents, the two people she'd trusted most, should have been able to trust above all others, had kept something so important a secret from her? Especially when they'd always been so honest about everything else? At least, she'd thought they had. What if they'd kept other secrets too? Ugh… What if Adam was keeping secrets from her? Because she was pretty sure he hadn't told her everything.

She sighed. It wasn't fair to blame Adam when he

seemed to have her and the baby's best interests at heart. Her parents had had her whole life to explain she was adopted. Adam had been in her life for less than twelve hours. All of which they'd been on the run for their lives. And he needed her to trust him. Well...she couldn't give him her full trust just yet—he'd have to earn that—but she could cooperate.

Adam stepped into the doorway with the bags and gestured her forward.

She smiled at him.

His answering smile had some of the ice melting from her heart. They'd get through this. They had no choice, really.

While he stood watch, she hurried down the steps and walkway, swung the car door open and got in. Scanning the immediate area for any threats, she stuck the key in the ignition and turned. It clicked but didn't turn over. Her heart stopped in that instant, and she dove from the car.

"Get out!" Adam tossed the bags back into the house and bolted toward her.

The world behind her exploded. A wall of heat slammed into her back and threw her against the porch railing. She hit it hard and dropped. Darkness crept in, tunneled her vision. The odor of singed hair followed her into oblivion.

Adam reached Jaelyn an instant after she dropped to the ground. He lifted her over his shoulder and carried her inside. He slammed the door shut behind him with his foot, lowered her to the ground beside the bags he'd dropped, and turned the deadbolt. "Jaelyn, get up. Now."

"Huh?" Her eyelids fluttered open, her eyes dazed and unfocused.

"You have to get up." He eased her up, hooked the diaper bag cross body, then got her to her feet. "We have to run. Now."

She nodded, clearly not fully aware of what was going on around her. Under any other circumstances, he'd have left her where she fell and called an ambulance while administering first aid. But these weren't other circumstances. Whoever had planted the car bomb was most likely lying in wait somewhere on the driveway, had probably watched her narrow escape. Bile burned the back of his throat at the memory, the instant he'd realized why the car didn't turn over.

Jaelyn staggered toward the couch, scooped the infant seat from the floor over her elbow.

Adam grabbed the briefcase. Since it had a weapon in it as well as the evidence he'd need to get Alessandra's killer, he couldn't leave it behind. Then he grabbed Jaelyn's bag so no one could ID her. He'd have to leave his own bag. It didn't matter. His wallet with his ID was in his pocket, so they couldn't identify him through the bag. He shoved one of the guns he'd taken from Maya's briefcase into Jaelyn's hand. "Do you know how to use this?"

She stared at the weapon and shook her head. Then she clutched his arm in a vicelike grip as her eyes started to roll back.

"Hey." He shook her, once, tapped her cheek. "Look at me."

When her eyes refocused, he grabbed the hand she held the gun in. "You just point and shoot. Got it?"

"Yeah." Rather than nodding, she kept her head perfectly still.

"Okay, I'll go first, then you follow." He started across the house toward the back. No way could he chance running into the woods without knowing how many assassins might be lying in wait or where they were positioned.

"Where are you going? There's nothing out there but ocean."

"We'll head for the woods." If they could make it down the beach without getting killed. Their only advantage was the fact that their pursuers would probably waste time searching the house before coming after them. "Go to the right."

He flung the back door open, gave one quick look around, then bolted.

To her credit, as dazed and disoriented as she was, Jaclyn kept pace, the baby's seat clutched tightly against her. Maybe he should have taken the seat? No. He needed to be able to drop everything and get his hands free at a moment's notice in case he had to fight.

In some part of him, deep inside where he didn't dare look too closely, he knew he was lying to himself. Knew the real reason he couldn't carry the child, could barely even look at her, was because she reminded him too much of what he'd lost. Even as he ran, the memory plowed into him—Alessandra, her cheeks glowing, eyes filled with tears of joy, as she told him the news, shared that he was going to be a father.

Senator Mark Lowell had denied him that privilege when Adam had gotten too close to the truth, and the senator had ordered the hit on his wife, months before his child would have taken its first breath. His throat closed. Rage surged through him, begged him to turn and confront their pursuers.

"Adam." The fear in Jaelyn's voice tugged him back. "They're following, coming around both sides of the house."

The flashlight beams made their pursuers easy enough to spot, but did he really want to risk a shoot-out with Jaelyn half out of it and an infant to consider? Or would it be better to try to disappear under the cover of darkness the thick stand of pine trees would provide?

He reached the shelter of the woods a step before her, then braced himself to shoot, to cover her retreat with the child. He waited until she was behind him then whirled on the men moving across the beach toward them. When one of them yelled and gestured in their direction with his light, Adam fired off two warning shots.

The beams scattered as their pursuers dove for cover.

Jaelyn paused and glanced back over her shoulder. "Aren't you coming?"

Violent tremors tore through him. With the diaper bag across his body, Jaelyn's bag over one shoulder, the briefcase in his hand, and the closely spaced, mature pine trees closing in on him, he felt like he was going to suffocate. He wanted desperately to go back out onto the beach, to confront the coming threat, to demand answers as to why his wife and child were taken from him.

"Adam?" Jaelyn lay a hand on his shoulder.

No way could he risk two lives. They had to run, had to hide, no matter how badly he wanted to make a stand. If they could keep ahead of their pursuers, gain some kind of lead, they'd be home free. Maybe.

"Go." Letting go of the past, for now, he stuffed the gun into his pocket and followed Jaelyn deeper into the woods. It was the best…the only…option they had. "Don't go straight."

She angled toward the beach instantly. It was probably a smart move, since their pursuers would expect them to try to reach a road. Jaelyn moved fast, weaving between trees and brush, despite the cumbersome infant seat. She stayed just inside the tree line with the beach in sight.

Again, Adam agreed. If they headed deeper into the woods, there was a good chance they'd end up lost before they could find help.

"What about the men coming after us?" Jaelyn's teeth chattered.

"Ignore them. They'll either catch us or they won't." They'd deal with it if the time came. In the meantime, hopefully, he and Jaelyn could move fast enough to disappear into the cover of darkness. The increasing storm could work to their advantage, muffle their footsteps, provide an additional layer of protection.

The wind picked up, whipping through the pine stand, driving the ice-cold rain into their faces. The rumble of crashing waves, one after another pounding against the shore, drowned out all other sound, so he had no idea how close their pursuers were, only that they would come.

Jaelyn tilted the seat toward her body, ran hunched over trying to protect the baby from the worst of the storm.

Then the child let out a cry, long, loud and distressed.

Jaelyn stumbled, went down hard on one knee.

Panic assailed him. When he reached her, he fell to his knees by her side.

She was breathing hard, soaked from the rain.

The baby continued to cry, deep, wracking sobs. Even the cover of the storm wouldn't be able to completely drown out the sound. They had to get her out of the seat.

Jaelyn's hands shook as she tried to unbuckle the strap. She needed help. Even if she could manage to work the buckle, she was in no condition to carry the little girl. He was going to have to take the baby from her.

Jaelyn had asked him earlier if he believed in God, and he'd said he didn't know, which was true enough. He wasn't sure if God didn't exist or if He'd simply abandoned Adam when he'd begged for Alessandra and his child to be saved. But if God did exist, then it wasn't true what they said—that God didn't give you more than you could handle. Because of everything that had been asked of Adam over the past five years, this was the one thing he couldn't do. How could he bear the responsibility for this child when he'd failed his own child so completely?

He couldn't.

His breath came in short gasps as he struggled for air, sucking in deep gulps of salt and brine.

"Adam!" Jaelyn managed to free the baby. "We have to go! Now!"

"Wait." He lay a hand on hers to keep her from lifting the child from the seat, then thrust her bag toward her and handed her the briefcase. "I'll take her."

"Are you sure?"

"Yeah." He nodded, about as far from sure as he'd ever been about anything in his life, and lifted the tiny bundle into his arms. "Just go."

She focused on him for another moment, studied him while he kept his expression carefully neutral, then staggered to her feet. She took off her raincoat and wrapped it around the baby, then lay a gentle kiss on top of her head before she turned and started forward again.

"God help us," he whispered and, tucking the baby tighter against his body, he started to move.

The little girl cried beneath Jaelyn's raincoat, deep, racking sobs he'd do anything to soothe, and yet, the sound brought comfort with the knowledge she was alive. It also brought fear that her cries would give away their position. How could he fight now with the baby in his arms? He began to second-guess his decision to carry her, then watched as Jaelyn tripped, fumbled the briefcase, and barely managed to regain her footing. No, he had no choice, but God help him, he would not lose this child. He would find a way to protect her somehow.

They moved through the woods as night inched closer to morning. He kept a firm hold on the child, his fingers a mass of pins and needles before going blessedly numb. The rain finally gave up its relentless pounding, but the cold seeped all the way through him.

When the baby's cries finally eased, he sucked in a deep breath and glanced over his shoulder. Darkness swallowed the woods, surrounded them, cocooned them in its embrace. Silence descended.

Then he uttered the first prayer he'd said in five long

years, "Thank you for saving us, and please let this baby be okay."

Tremors shook his hand as he lifted the corner of Jaelyn's raincoat.

The infant looked up at him, eyes wide and red rimmed, filled with fear. But she was safe.

He closed his eyes for one blessed moment. "Oh, God, thank you."

They trudged on as hints of gray teased the horizon, as the sun struggled to peek through the thick cloud cover onto the endless expanse of ocean.

The baby remained quiet and still, so he peeked at her again and had a moment of panic when he found her eyes closed, but a quick check showed she was breathing. Exhaustion from crying, fear, and the smooth rocking motion of his walking must have lulled her to sleep. He covered her again, to keep her as warm and dry as possible, but they needed to get to help. None of them were dressed for the weather, especially since they were soaked through.

Though he could see the outline of the beach through the trees, make out the silhouettes of homes that lined the shore, he had no idea how far they'd traveled, nor if the homes he could see would have residents or be uninhabited at this time of year. It didn't matter. He'd break in if need be. "We have to get to help, Jaelyn."

She nodded, her attention fully riveted in front of her as they finally emerged from the span of woods.

Once he reached the dunes that were barely holding back the higher-than-normal tide, he wrapped the raincoat around Jaelyn's shoulders, unzipped his jacket and tucked the baby inside, close to his heart for warmth. Then he collapsed to his knees. When Jaelyn fell to her knees on the sand beside him, he gathered her close, cradling the baby between them, and rested his cheek on her head.

He had no idea how they'd made it, where they'd found the strength or the courage to keep on going, but he offered a prayer of thanks. Then he did what he should have done five years ago and wasn't able to do after losing Alessandra and the baby, he prayed for his wife and their unborn child, prayed they were safe and happy with God and that he'd one day see them again. While the ocean raged, and a flock of seagulls screamed and dove, he closed his eyes and wept.

# SIX

Jaelyn drifted in some strange place between sleep and wakefulness, between consciousness and unconsciousness. Snuggled against Adam, with the baby between them, she was no longer cold, no longer shivering. Some deep part of her screamed a warning, but she couldn't quite grasp what was wrong, and her eyes fluttered closed.

"Hey!"

Though she could make out the word, she had no idea who was speaking. A male voice. Adam?

"Hey, there!"

No, not Adam. Too far away. Adam was beside her. She could feel the weight of his arm across her back, feel the warmth emanating from him.

"Are you guys okay?" That voice again, impatient, insistent.

She struggled to open her eyes, managed to get one barely open, and found an older gentleman bent over, hands on his knees, inches from her face.

"Oh, man, thank God. I thought maybe you guys were, you know…dead or something."

Jaelyn lifted her head to look at Adam, and every muscle in her body screamed in protest.

A hand gripped her arm, gentle but insistent. "We have to get you inside now. My wife, she's waiting for me to come back in. She wanted to call nine-one-one, but I told her I'd check things out first."

At the mention of calling the authorities, her eyes shot open.

The man straightened. "If I'm not back in a few minutes, though, she won't be able to resist the urge."

Jaelyn tried to tell him they were okay, that they didn't need the police, but all that came out was a harsh rasp and then she started to cough. Pain racked her body.

The man pounded on her back.

When the fit subsided, she wheezed in a breath and lifted her gaze to Adam.

He shifted, looked into her eyes.

And in that one moment, she was so grateful they were alive she wanted to grab the sides of his face, yank his mouth down to hers, and plant a great big kiss right smack on him. Thankfully, she came to her senses before she could follow through. Instead, she lay a hand against his cheek. "You okay?"

"Yeah, but we have to get up, need to get somewhere dry and warm." And safe. Though he didn't add that in front of the new arrival, she could read it in his eyes. He tilted his face into her hand for just a moment, closed his eyes.

And there was so much she wanted to say to him. She wanted to reassure him they'd make it through this, wanted to thank him for keeping them safe so far, for not abandoning her, or Maya, or the baby. She wanted to ask if he was really okay. He seemed fine physically, alert, coherent, but shaky. Shaky seemed to fit his emotional state as well. But now wasn't the time for questions. They had to move.

Every instinct she had begged her to trust him, and yet… She lowered her hand, struggled to her feet with the help of the stranger who'd come to their aid.

When her legs threatened to buckle, she willed them to stay strong, to stop shaking, and she held her arms out for the baby.

Adam handed her over.

And the stranger gasped. "Oh, my, you need to come with me right now."

Jaelyn hugged the baby against her, kissed the top of her head, covered her ice-cold hands with one of her own.

"I'm Hank, by the way." He reached out a hand and helped Adam to his feet. If he had any opinion about the two of them being out on the beach with a baby in tow, soaked to the bone, he kept it to himself. "You folks in some sort of trouble?"

The man's southern accent was enough to tell her he wasn't a local but probably came up north to spend the holidays in his summer home. At this point, that would have to be reason enough to trust him.

"We're okay." Adam braced himself for a moment, then straightened and lifted the briefcase. "But we'd really appreciate it if we could use your phone to call a friend to pick us up."

"Sure, sure."

"Thank you," Jaelyn said. If they could just get off the beach, maybe no one would know where they'd gone.

Hank looked out over the ocean then clapped Adam on the back. "Come on then. I can do even better than just the phone. I'll wrangle up a nice hot cup of coffee for each of you while you're waitin' on your friend. Could be Martha might even be talked into cookin' up some breakfast."

"That would be amazing, thank you." The thought of a nice warm mug to wrap her hands around almost made Jaelyn weep.

"Sure, thing." He winked. "Oh, and Merry Christmas to ya."

"Yes, Merry Christmas." Jaelyn hugged the baby closer, reflecting on the hours they'd spent struggling on the run and so thankful they'd survived the night and had been found by someone so willing to offer help. She'd witnessed the worst side of humanity over the past twelve hours. It was refreshing to now witness the best.

Adam took her hand as they trudged up the beach, and she was grateful for the gesture of support, for the warmth, for the sense of camaraderie his touch evoked.

Hank led them across a wide expanse of back deck that boasted an incredible view of the beach, then through a small back door, and into the mudroom of a cozy bungalow. The scent of cinnamon and sugar filled the air, and Jaelyn's stomach turned over.

"Oh, my." An older woman dressed in black slacks and a red blouse rushed in carrying a stack of towels. Her gray hair was tied into a neat bun at the back of her head, and she wore red ball ornament earrings, despite the ridiculously early hour. "Here you go. Get dried off now, and we'll try to find something for you to wear."

"Thank you." Jaelyn took one of the towels she offered and wrapped the baby. After a moment's hesitation, she handed her to the woman so she could dry herself off. "Do you have somewhere I could change the baby? I want to get her out of these wet clothes as soon as possible."

Despite the fact she'd been covered by the raincoat for some of the night, enough water had still seeped in and soaked her blanket and pajamas.

Adam held out the dripping diaper bag, and she noticed he still clutched the waterlogged briefcase in a white-knuckled grip. The fact that he'd maintained a death grip on the briefcase with one of Maya's guns still inside it wasn't lost on her. Her own bag, however, with Maya's purse and Jaelyn's cell phone and ID inside must have been lost.

She remembered him handing it to her when he took the baby from her, but she couldn't recall what had happened to it. She must have dropped it somewhere along the way. Great. Now if the gunmen searching for them found it, they'd know about Jaelyn—if they didn't already.

She took the diaper bag from him, slung it over her shoulder, and took the baby back from the woman. "Thank you."

"Of course, of course. Come with me." She started out of the room, a whirlwind of motion, probably brought on by nerves. "I'm Martha, by the way."

She paused, waited.

# "One Minute" Survey

## You get up to **FOUR** books <u>and</u> a Mystery Gift...

**YOU** pick your books –
**WE** pay for everything.
You get up to FOUR new books and a Mystery Gift...
absolutely FREE!
**Total retail value: Over $20!**

Dear Reader,

Your opinions are important to us. So if you'll participate in our fast and free "One Minute" Survey, YOU can pick up to four wonderful books that WE pay for when you try the Harlequin Reader Service!

As a leading publisher of women's fiction, we'd love to hear from you. That's why we promise to reward you for completing our survey.

IMPORTANT: Please complete the survey and return it. We'll send your Free Books and a Free Mystery Gift right away. And we pay for shipping and handling too! *We pay for EVERYTHING!*

Try **Love Inspired® Romance Larger-Print** and get 2 books and fall in love with inspirational romances that take you on an uplifting journey of faith, forgiveness and hope.

Try **Love Inspired® Suspense Larger-Pri**nt and get 2 books where courage and optimism unite in stories of faith and love in the face of danger.

**Or TRY BOTH!**

Thank you again for participating in our "One Minute" Survey. It really takes just a minute (or less) to complete the survey… and your free books and gift will be well worth it!

If you continue with your subscription, you can look forward to curated monthly shipments of brand-new books from your selected series, always at a discount off the cover price! Plus you can cancel any time. So don't miss out, return your One Minute Survey today to get your Free books.

*Pam Powers*

# "One Minute" Survey

## GET YOUR FREE BOOKS AND A FREE GIFT!
✓ Complete this Survey ✓ Return this survey

▶ DETACH AND MAIL CARD TODAY! ▶

**1** Do you try to find time to read every day?
☐ YES ☐ NO

**2** Do you prefer books which reflect Christian values?
☐ YES ☐ NO

**3** Do you enjoy having books delivered to your home?
☐ YES ☐ NO

**4** Do you share your favorite books with friends?
☐ YES ☐ NO

**YES!** I have completed the above "One Minute" Survey. Please send me my Free Books and a Free Mystery Gift (worth over $20 retail). I understand that I am under no obligation to buy anything, as explained on the back of this card.

☐ **Love Inspired® Romance Larger-Print**
122/322 CTI G2AK

☐ **Love Inspired® Suspense Larger-Print**
107/307 CTI G2AK

☐ **BOTH**
122/322 & 107/307 CTI G2AL

FIRST NAME | LAST NAME

ADDRESS

APT.# | CITY

STATE/PROV. | ZIP/POSTAL CODE

EMAIL ☐ Please check this box if you would like to receive newsletters and promotional emails from Harlequin Enterprises ULC and its affiliates. You can unsubscribe anytime.

LI/LIS-1123-OM

Jaelyn glanced at Adam as they followed the woman through a large living room. A Christmas tree stood sentinel in one corner. The pile of gifts beneath it, many wrapped in children's paper, combined with Martha's guest-ready attire, renewed Jaelyn's sense of urgency. If these people were expecting guests for the holiday, they had to get out of there. The fewer people who saw them, the better. If their attackers somehow found them, she didn't want these people who'd shown them such kindness put in a killer's crosshairs.

"I'm Jack, and this is Suzie." Adam gripped Jaelyn's hand, squeezed. "We're very grateful for your help, ma'am. We're not from around here, were just visiting for the holiday and had a minor accident during the night. The storm had let up, so we thought we could just walk down the beach until we came to a town, but we got caught up in a squall."

Jaelyn just smiled. While she understood Adam only sought to protect the people who'd so graciously opened their home to them, she didn't like the idea of deceiving them any more than she liked the thought of putting them in harm's way. They really needed to go.

"And this is our little girl, Carly."

"Oh, she's a beauty," Martha cooed. "But the poor thing must be half frozen."

"I know. I feel awful about that. I don't know what we were thinking." Despite the fact the story Adam wove was mostly fiction, the regret in his voice struck Jaelyn as sincere.

"Here you go." Martha gestured toward a small bedroom with two twin-size beds, a couple of dressers, and a door that led to a connecting bathroom. The lack of any personal effects told Jaelyn it was probably a guest suite. "You go ahead and change the baby, then look in the dresser drawers for something dry for yourself. My daughter leaves clothes in there for when she visits, and there are more dry towels in the linen closet in the bathroom."

"Thank you so much, Martha."

"Sure." She started to close the door behind her, then turned. "Oh, and I have a batch of cinnamon rolls coming out of the oven, so you'll share breakfast and coffee with us, I hope."

"We'd love to, thank you." Adam lay a hand on Martha's back, then led her into the hallway and pulled the door shut behind them, leaving Jaelyn alone with the baby.

She quickly stripped off the baby's wet pajamas, dried her with a towel, and did a fast but thorough exam. She seemed okay, quiet but responsive. Once she had her diaper changed, she took a blanket from the bottom of the bed and wrapped her, then set her against a pillow in the middle of the bed where she'd be safe. She was suddenly struck by the realization that she didn't even know if the baby could roll over on her own yet, though she doubted it.

With her little ward warm and secure, Jaelyn unzipped the bag, prepared a bottle, and used one of the towels Martha had left with her to prop the bottle so she could drink. As much as she'd love to snuggle the baby close, she had to get dry first.

But, before that, she pulled the gun Adam had given

her from the back of her waistband. It had to be soaked, but since she knew nothing about weapons, she had no clue if that meant it wouldn't still work. She set it aside on the dresser.

A quick search through the drawers unearthed a pair of black leggings and an oversize pale pink sweatshirt, which she donned quickly along with a pair of thick pink socks once she'd dried off. Since there were no shoes to borrow, she'd have to put her wet ones back on when they left, but she was grateful for the warmth of the dry clothes and the feeling beginning to return to her extremities.

She began to shiver and wrapped a blanket from the bottom of the second bed around her shoulders, then sat beside the baby. She ran a hand over her soft, dark peach fuzz. "I'm sorry you were frightened, little one. I'll try to do better to keep you out of danger, but no matter what, I promise I will keep you safe."

She wiped the tears that tracked a steady stream down her raw cheeks—there was no time to indulge—and pulled the diaper bag closer. Daggers shot through her fingers as she emptied the bag onto the bed in search of dry pajamas and to take stock.

Thankfully, Adam had had the sense to zip the bag and it seemed waterproof. While some water had managed to seep in, almost everything was dry. They should have enough bottles to last the day and night, but they'd have to find a way to restock the next day. The same went for diapers. She searched through a handful of pajamas for the warmest pair, then set them aside. Once she had herself somewhat organized, had regained a sense of control she had no doubt was nothing more than an illusion, she took a deep breath. She'd just dry out the bag, tuck the gun beneath the baby's things, and get back to Adam so they could get out of there.

Using the towel she'd dried herself with, she soaked up what water had seeped into the bag, then lifted out the bottom piece to dry underneath it. Her breath caught. In the bottom of the bag lay a small leather journal. Jaelyn lifted the book, opened the first page.

Written in neat cursive was the name *Leigha Barlowe* followed by a date two months earlier and the numbers 7-6 19. Another date? Could be. Or could it mean seven pounds six ounces? Nineteen inches? She flipped through the remaining pages, what seemed to be a detailed log of Maya's pregnancy on cursory examination.

If this could be used as proof that Maya had given birth to the child, perhaps Adam could find a relative to care for her until this was over. But would she be safe with someone else? Safer than she was with Jaelyn and Adam? Jaelyn didn't know if Maya had family. What if they could only find a paternal grandparent? One who might turn the baby over to the Hunter? Maybe the best thing to do would be to turn the baby over to Gabe, or at least see what options he could offer.

On the last page was a detailed recounting of her delivery, at home, with a midwife in attendance and no complications. But something intruded on her optimism. It began as a small niggle at the back of her neck. Something wasn't right. Where was the baby's birth certificate? Surely, Maya would have secreted it with the journal. She checked the inside of the front and back covers. Nothing. Holding the book open over the bed, she turned it upside down, thumbed the pages, shook it. A folded piece of paper fell out.

Jaelyn's hands shook as she lifted it, opened it. It was the birth certificate she'd been hoping to find, but instead of the name Leigha Barlowe as she'd expected, it read Leigha Reed. Jaelyn's name was listed as her mother. And no father was listed.

The room did one slow, stomach-pitching spin. She dropped the book and the document and splayed her hands against the bed, bracing herself to keep the world straight. She sucked in a few deep breaths. What was going on? Had Maya hoped to contact Jaelyn and ask her to keep the child? Had she expected Jaelyn to take the baby and go on the run?

The baby's cries tore her attention from the chaotic whirlwind her mind had become. After pausing for a moment to be sure the vertigo had passed, she lifted the child into her arms, stroked a finger along the side of her cheek. "Hush now, little one. We're going to find Adam, and I'll take care of you."

She cried louder.

Jaelyn was still shaky, whether from the ordeal they'd suffered through the night, the implications of the journal she'd found, or the fact that according to the document lying facedown beside her on the bed, this child belonged to her, she didn't know. She leaned back against the headboard, picked up the bottle that had rolled off the towel, and cuddled the baby close. The instant Jaelyn put the bottle back into her mouth, she sucked greedily, wrapped one tiny fist around Jaelyn's pinky. "It's okay, Leigha, rest now. Aunt Jaelyn will take care of you."

When she glanced down at the journal lying on the bed, back cover open, her gaze settled on the final entry, and a chill raced through her.

*Time for Leigha to disappear.*

Adam stuffed his wet, pretty much ruined clothes into a small garbage bag he'd found beneath the bathroom sink. Like many of the summer homes dotting Long Island, this one boasted mostly suites, with each bedroom having its own bathroom and sitting area for guests or families' convenience.

He cinched the belt Martha had given him one notch tighter. She had a good eye for size and had said her son-in-law's jeans would only be a little big on him, and she'd been spot on. The long-sleeved Henley and flannel shirt he wore over it fit perfectly. Unfortunately, he'd have to stuff his feet back into his own waterlogged shoes when it was time to go—he glanced at his watch—which needed to be soon.

While he didn't want to linger too long with Hank and Martha, desperate to keep danger from coming to their door, they had to wait for Pat to arrive. Before changing, he'd used the landline to call Seaport Fire and Rescue. Thankfully, Pat had been there and was supposedly on his way after a quick stop to pick up a car seat for the baby.

His heart stuttered at the thought of the infant. He'd had such a difficult time with her in the beginning, couldn't even look at her. Not because he didn't like children—he actually did—but because he'd been so afraid to fail her. Every time his gaze landed on her, it was a reminder that she might die on his watch, that he might not be able to protect her. But now, all he wanted was to get back to her, see her, touch her, assure himself she was safe. The fact that they'd almost walked out of Maya's room before they'd found her knotted his gut. What would have happened to her?

He did a mental head shake to clear his mind, had to if he was going to think clearly enough to function and get them out of this mess. Though the guilt he suffered had him shouldering the blame for their current situation, he knew it wasn't all his doing. Or was it? If he hadn't gone after the corrupt senator five years ago when a junior partner at Adam's firm had insisted she believed he was hiring hits, after the same woman had been accosted, would any of them be in the position they were in right now?

Would Alessandra and his child still be with him? He had no way to know that. No way to know what might have become of them under different circumstances. He'd done what he felt was right, and Alessandra had supported him completely, had encouraged him to do the right thing and try to stop the senator from hiring out any more hits. Neither of them could have anticipated the outcome…that she'd end up at the top of his list.

Perhaps it was time to stop dwelling on a past he couldn't change and start looking toward his future, a concept he hadn't dared consider for five long years. He'd been alone for all of that time, had pushed away his friends, his coworkers. Even Alessandra's family, who'd so kindly reached out to him, embraced him, offered their forgiveness and their love. And he'd been without God. He'd never been overly religious, but he'd believed in God, prayed regularly, maybe not traditional prayers, but more of an ongoing conversation. And then, when he'd shut everyone else out of his life, he'd turned away from God too, and had lived with silence.

Well, he wouldn't turn Jaelyn away, nor would he abandon the child before he saw them safe. And to do that, he needed answers. He picked up the phone on the bedside table to make a call, then winced when his paralegal, Carrie, answered with a cheery, "Merry Christmas."

How could he have forgotten? He apologized profusely, but she'd been with him a long time, knew the case he was working on, so she'd understand. He asked her to do the research he needed, the next day, of course, wished her a Merry Christmas, and ended the call hoping the research would pay off. And in the meantime, it was time to get moving.

He raked a hand through his still damp hair. He'd already checked the contents of the briefcase, found everything to be surprisingly dry, including the weapon still inside. He hadn't asked Jaelyn if she still had the gun that he'd given her as they'd fled. He wrapped his own in a plastic bag and put it in the briefcase, then tucked Maya's remaining handgun into the waistband of his jeans. He checked in the mirror that his flannel shirt covered it. Satisfied that no one would notice the weapon, he closed and locked the briefcase then grabbed it and the bag containing his clothes and walked into the kitchen.

Martha pulled two trays of cinnamon buns from the oven and turned. She smiled when she saw him. "Be a dear, would you, and grab me one of the platters from the cabinet above the stove?"

"Sure thing, ma'am." He did as she asked, set the platter on the butcher block countertop beside the stove while she started loosening the buns with a spatula. "I just wanted to thank you again for taking us in this morning, for everything you've done for us."

"Of course, dear. I'm quite sure under similar circumstances you'd do the same for us." She paused a moment to pat the back of the hand he'd left resting on the counter. Something flickered over her expression that had him wondering if she truly bought their cover story or if she suspected there was more to it. His gut told him it was the latter.

"I would, yes, and if there's ever anything you need from me, I'd be more than happy to help." Of course, once he walked out without giving Hank and Martha his real name, they'd never be able to contact him even if they did need help. When this was all over and it was safe to do so, he'd return to the house on the beach and bring back the clothing they'd borrowed, and then he'd tell them the truth, let them know just how much their generosity had meant to him, that their kindness had saved all of their lives. But for now, well, remaining anonymous was the kindest thing he could do for them.

She smiled knowingly and returned to piling over-size cinnamon buns on the platter. "I've already set the coffee out in the living room. I thought it would be nicer to sit in there with the fire to keep us warm. You go ahead and make yourself at home, and I'll be right along with these as soon as I frost them."

"Thank you." Adam scanned the empty beach through the French doors then did as instructed. He found Hank already sitting in an oversize chair, one ankle propped on his knee, sipping coffee, his ruddy complexion made more flushed by the fire and the hot drink.

Cozy seating arrangements dotted a homey room meant for entertaining. A bar in one corner held coffee and tea machines along with baskets filled with individual-sized snacks. Adam's stomach growled, and he lay his hand against it, suddenly realizing he was starving.

"Don't just stand there, boy, come on in and take a load off." Hank gestured to the chair beside him. "Grab yourself a mug of coffee."

Adam grinned. He'd never had a close family. His mother had lost her parents when Adam was a child and he'd never known his father's parents, since his father had walked out on him and his mother when he was too young to remember. If he'd grown up with grandparents, he'd have wanted them to be just like Hank and Martha. "Thank you, sir."

"Sure, sure." He waved him toward the chair. "And you can stop with all the sir and ma'am—we're just Hank and Martha."

Adam took a mug from the tray on the coffee table, filled it with coffee from the urn, inhaled deeply the rich aroma, and sat with Hank.

The older man studied him for a moment then set his mug down and sighed. "I'm not one to pry, son, but I can't help gettin' the feelin' you and your missus are in some serious trouble."

Yikes. He lowered his gaze to the steam wafting from the mug cradled between his hands. While he might have enjoyed having a grandfather like Hank, having him as a dad would have been rough. Adam had a feeling his kids didn't get away with much.

"Now, I won't ask what it is, but I will say, before the women join us, if you need help, you've only to ask." He gripped Adam's wrist, squeezed in a gentle offer of support, then lifted his mug. "And that's all I'll say about that."

Adam found himself wanting to blurt out the entire story, unburden himself on this man he had a strong suspicion would simply sit and listen, then offer some sage advice that would answer all his questions, alleviate all his doubts. Instead, he looked Hank in the eye and nodded. "Thank you. I can't tell you how much I appreciate everything you've already done."

"Of course." His pale blue eyes sparkled when he smiled. "What better day to be blessed with the ability to help another?"

"Cinnamon buns are ready." Martha walked into the room carrying an overloaded platter, and Adam jumped up to take it from her and set it on the coffee table. "Thank you, son."

It wasn't lost on him that Hank and Martha continuously called him son or boy, anything but the fake name he'd given them when they'd met. No, not much snuck past these two.

"Now sit, eat, enjoy. I'm just going to knock on the bedroom door and let your woman know breakfast is here if she's hungry."

"I'm here, Martha." Jaelyn walked in looking refreshed. She set the diaper bag beside a love seat, along with a plastic bag he assumed contained her wet clothing, then she sat in the corner of the love seat with the baby cradled close. "Thank you."

"Here, let me get you coffee." Adam set his mug on a side table and stood, poured Jaelyn a mug, then handed it to her. He leaned close and whispered, "You okay?"

She nodded, her cheek soft against his, and whispered back, "Leigha."

His gaze shot to the baby in her arms, snoring softly as she slept. The name suited her, soft, beautiful, delicate. He smiled into Jaelyn's eyes as he pulled back.

As they all sat there, Martha beside Jaelyn where she could keep stealing glances at Leigha, occasionally stroking a hand over her dark hair, Adam had a moment to envision Hank and Martha sitting in this room with their own children while their grandchildren ran and played. He had no doubt theirs was a home filled with love and joy, and for just a moment, he coveted that, even wondered if this was Jaelyn's dream. And then he came to his senses.

What was he thinking?

He scrubbed a hand over scruff that had long ago passed five o'clock shadow and shook his head to rid himself of the vision.

As they shared cinnamon buns and coffee, Hank and Martha entertained them with stories about their children, their grandchildren—all thirteen of them and the two on the way—and asked not a single question about Adam or Jaelyn. And he couldn't be more grateful to them.

Footsteps intruded on their conversation, loud, more than one set, and coming from the back deck.

Jaelyn stared at Adam, her eyes wide and filled with fear.

Adam went on alert. He lurched to his feet. No way Pat would come around the back. Plus, it was too soon for him to have arrived. "Are you expecting company?"

Hank stood, his gaze narrowed on Adam. "Not until later when the kids come out from the city."

Jaelyn surged to her feet, clutched the baby tightly against her, looked around the room as if searching for an escape route.

But there was no escape. They were caged, like cornered animals. Adam strode to the front windows, peeked out the blinds.

A black sedan sat in the driveway, and two men beside it scanned the area.

"Two on the back deck, peeking in the windows," Hank said from right behind him.

If they'd settled in the kitchen for breakfast, they'd all probably be dead already. As it was, maybe they'd live long enough to feel the terror of knowing they were about to die.

# SEVEN

Jaelyn stood where she was, trapped. Claustrophobia assailed her. They had to get out, but there was no way out. If they moved from where they were, they'd be visible through the back windows to whoever was creeping around the back deck. She never should have stuffed the gun Adam had given her in the diaper bag, should have kept it with her instead. Even the illusion of safety would be better than the sheer terror she now experienced. Maybe she should hand the baby over to Martha and go for the weapon.

She looked down at Leigha, so serene in sleep, her features so delicate, the dark peach fuzz a sharp contrast against her nearly translucent skin. No. She couldn't do it, couldn't hand her over to anyone else.

Adam reached behind him for the gun stuffed in his waistband.

Hank lay a hand on his arm. "Just wait."

Adam hesitated, looked Hank in the eye. "I'm sorry for this. Sorry we brought trouble to your door."

"Did the two of you do anything wrong?"

"No, sir, we did not."

"Well then, seems you didn't bring the trouble, now, did you?" Without waiting for an answer, he gestured for Adam to stand beside the front door, then pointed to Jaelyn and Martha on his way out of the room. "You two ladies get down behind the couch, try to keep the baby from waking up and crying if you can."

Jaelyn nodded, crouched behind the couch ready to spring up at a moment's notice if necessary, and willed herself to calm down, to ease her grip on Leigha before she woke her.

Martha ducked beside her and threaded her fingers through Jaelyn's, held her hand in a firm, steady grip.

Grateful for the support, Jaelyn gripped her hand back, lay her head against Martha's for just a moment, then shifted Leigha into Martha's arms. Jaelyn kissed the baby's head. There was no choice. She needed her hands free in case she had to fight. And she would fight, to the death if necessary, to save this child and the people who'd so kindly taken them in. To save Adam, who—despite the secrets he clearly harbored—had repeatedly risked his life to save them. She whispered to Martha, "If anything happens to me, take Leigha to Seaport Fire and Rescue. Explain what happened and tell them Jaelyn sent you. They'll take care of her."

Martha nodded. The woman sat with her back against the couch and kissed the baby's head, then hunched over her to shield her.

Someone knocked on the front door, brisk, insistent.

When Jaelyn peered over the couch, her gaze met Adam's. A million things passed between them—fear, regret, determination. She eyed the diaper bag, not so far and yet a million miles away. Her entire body vibrated as she crouched, held her breath, waited.

And then, Hank was back. He hurried across the room and shoved a shotgun into Adam's hands, then held up a hand for him to stay behind the door.

Jaelyn dropped back below the couch as he opened the door.

"Good mornin' to ya," Hank greeted.

"Morning."

Jaelyn held her breath, prayed Leigha wouldn't choose that moment to wake and cry.

"I'm sorry to bother you this morning," a man began, "but we're looking for a couple, a man and a woman, who are wanted in connection with a murder and escaped custody this morning. We have reason to believe they headed this way, and I noticed footprints on the stretch of beach out back, leading straight up to your back door. We just wanted to check and make sure everyone here is okay and there are no problems."

It wasn't lost on Jaelyn, and certainly wouldn't be on Hank, that they had not offered ID, nor had they identified the agency they supposedly worked for.

"Well, thank you, sir," Hank said. "Mighty nice of you to check in on us, but we've had no trouble here. My wife and my son and I just walked out to enjoy the sunrise, what there was of it anyway, what with all the gray and clouds."

If Jaelyn didn't know better, she'd believe him.

"Didn't see anyone, couple or otherwise, while we were out there. Sorry I couldn't be of more help, but if you want to leave a card, I'll be happy to get in touch if I do see anyone. Always willing to do my civic duty, after all."

Silence descended.

Jaelyn squeezed her eyes closed, willed the tremors coursing through her body to still. *Please, let them believe him. Please, let them believe him.*

"If you see them, lock your doors and don't open them. These two are armed and more dangerous than they look."

"I'll be sure to do that. Thank you again for the warning. I hope you find them."

At the sound of the door clicking closed, Jaelyn's breath shot from her lungs. She swiped her hands over her cheeks, shoving away tears she hadn't even realized had spilled over. And then Adam was there.

He held out a hand and helped her up.

Hank peered through the curtains until the men were gone, then took the shotgun from Adam, took a step back, and leveled the weapon at his chest. "Don't move."

Adam froze.

Martha gasped, then quickly looked down at Leigha sleeping in her arms.

"Martha, you bring that young 'un over here right now." He spoke without ever shifting his gaze from Adam's.

Frowning, first at her husband, then at Jaelyn, she did as he'd instructed, and Hank held out a hand to guide her behind him.

When Adam slowly lifted his hands to the sides, Jaelyn did the same, shifting a few inches to the right to allow both of them space if a fight was needed, though she desperately hoped they could defuse the situation without one.

"I hope you understand. I don't know who those men are, 'cept to know they're not who they're claimin' to be, but I don't know who either of you are either, and until I do, I can't in good conscience let you take this here baby out of this house."

"Hank..." Martha lay a hand on his shoulder from behind him.

"Don't you worry none, dear." He used the gun to gesture Adam toward the couch. "Now, as I see it, you have two choices. You can sit right down and give me the abbreviated version of why you had this infant out in the middle of the winter with those goons after you, and I'll do my best to help you out and see you safe, or you can take your woman—provided she'll go willingly with you—and walk out that door and Martha and I will see to the child's safety."

Adam kept his gaze leveled on Hank. "Listen to me, please. You're right, we're not who we claimed to be when we came in here, and I do apologize for deceiving you. It wasn't out of any malicious intent, that I can promise you. We just hoped to keep you safe and figured the more you knew, the more danger you'd be in."

"Well, now, while I do appreciate your concern, why don't you come clean and let me and the missus decide how much risk we're willing to take?"

"Fair enough." Keeping his hands where Hank could see them, he shifted toward the couch. "Can I please reach into my pocket for my wallet so I can show you my ID?"

He nodded once. "Slowly."

While Adam dipped a hand into his pocket, Jaelyn's heart pounded wildly. Blood rushed in her ears, drowning out the sound. They didn't have time for this. And she needed to get Leigha from Martha just in case those men returned and they had to make a run for it in a hurry. No way was she leaving the baby with a stranger, especially when their attackers had already found them. Who was to say they would follow Adam and Jaelyn? They could instead kill these people who'd so kindly taken them in and steal Leigha. And then an idea struck. "Please, if I may go to Leigha's diaper bag, I can prove she's my child."

Adam's shocked inhalation threw her for a moment, and she hoped Hank didn't notice.

He didn't seem to, as he nodded once. "But no games."

"No, sir. Thank you." She moved slowly, as Adam had, unzipped the bag, and for one instant she thought about grabbing the gun. What if Hank or Martha could tell the documents were forged? She shoved the thought ruthlessly aside. Grabbing the gun would be pointless. Not only might it be too waterlogged to work, but what was she going to do—shoot Hank? Martha? Instead, she slid the forged birth certificate out of the journal and held it out toward him. "My driver's license is in the briefcase, but Adam has the key. So if you don't mind him reaching into his pocket for it, I'll get that too."

Hank narrowed his gaze at her but nodded again.

While she quickly rummaged through the briefcase in search of the forged Montana driver's license, Adam held out his own ID for Hank's inspection.

He pursed his lips as he studied the documents, then gestured again toward the couch.

This time, Adam sat.

Jaelyn stood behind him and lay a hand on his shoulder. "Please, Hank, we appreciate you helping us so much, and I understand and appreciate your concern for Leigha, but the men who are after us already put my sister in the hospital, and they're coming for us. You have to let us go, and we must take Leigha with us or they will come for her."

With no choice if they wanted to get out of there without any violence, Adam gave him a quick recap of the past few days' events.

When he was done, Hank eased his grip on the shotgun, lowered it to his side. "Martha and I saw that mess at the hospital on the local news this morning. They said the gunman was going to recover but they didn't give any information about who he is."

Jaelyn inched forward and held her arms out for the baby.

When Martha glanced at Hank, he nodded, and she handed Leigha to Jaelyn.

Jaelyn tuned out everything going on around her, shifted her focus fully to the bundle in her arms. Though she ached to understand the truth of the situation that had sent her entire world into upheaval, the only thing that mattered in that instant was having Leigha back. Everything else could come later, and at that point, she had every intention of getting to the bottom of this whole mess. Starting with why her parents had never told her she was adopted and that she had a twin sister. Out of everything, that was the betrayal that stung the worst, even worse than Ronnie cheating on her when she'd needed him most.

"You folks need to get out of here before they come back." Hank set his shotgun aside and held a hand out to Adam.

Adam shook the man's hand even as he gripped Jaelyn's elbow and guided her toward the door. "I don't know how I can ever thank you for helping us, Hank, and I can't tell you how sorry I am that trouble followed us here."

Hank waved him off, peered around the corner so he could see out the French doors onto the back deck. "Don't worry about it. I'm just glad I found y'all when I did. And I hope you understand I needed answers before I could let you take that child outta here."

Adam turned to make eye contact with him, held his gaze. "I not only understand, but I appreciate your concern and your desire to do the right thing by her."

"Well, then, that's settled. Now we need to get you out of here. You can leave the bags with your wet clothes, just take what you need and come back for the rest another time when maybe we can sit out on the deck and you can share how this all turns out."

Adam nodded. "You bet we will, and thank you again."

Jaelyn hooked the diaper bag over her shoulder. "I'm so sorry, Martha."

The elderly woman swiped back a strand of hair that had come free from her bun then fussed over Leigha for a moment, tucking the blanket tighter around her.

"Don't you worry about a thing. You just keep this little one safe."

"Thank you. For everything A firefighter we know should be here any minute to pick us up. We just need to get out of the house and slip into the woods unnoticed."

"Okay, then." Hank nodded and held his hand out to his wife. "Come on, Martha. What do you say to a walk on the beach before the kids get here, draw the attention of anyone who might be watching?"

Her smile held such warmth when she looked at him, slid her hand into his, that Jaelyn's heart tripped. The memory of her parents came unbidden, her father holding a hand out to her mother, then his other out to Jaelyn—the picture-perfect happy family. How could they have kept the truth from her? Had they meant to tell her one day but had just run out of time? Pain tore through her. She'd trusted them so completely—would the sting of betrayal ever lessen?

She didn't have the answer to that, and probably only time would tell, so better to move on to more immediate problems, search for answers they could find. She had an idea how to get whoever was after Maya to come after them again, under controlled circumstances, but she had to make sure Leigha was somewhere safe before she mentioned it to Adam. And she needed time to compose her argument so he'd agree to using her as bait. They would lure the Hunter out of hiding and bring him and all of his associates to justice.

Adam held a branch aside for Jaelyn to pass with Leigha. The way she hovered protectively over the child touched him in a way nothing had for a long time. The sound of an engine running made him pause and listen. He lay a hand on her shoulder and gestured for her to duck behind a tree with the baby and wait for him to return. He leaned close to her and whispered against her ear, "If anything happens, run with the baby."

She nodded, her expression grim, and he wondered for a moment if she'd do as he asked or stay and try to fight if the need arose.

Leaving her to wait, he crouched low, crept closer to the edge of the wooded lot. A black Jeep idled at the curb, windows cracked, though not enough to see inside. The sun's glare blocked his view of the interior.

A light touch against the back of his shoulder had him practically jumping out of his skin.

"Sorry, I didn't mean to startle you." Jaelyn smiled apologetically. "It's safe. The Jeep is Jack's."

"You're sure?" He rubbed his chest where his heart thundered.

"I should be—it's new and he loves it. He's spent the past few weeks showing it to everyone who'd go out and take a look." She started to stand, but he gripped her wrist, held it.

"Please, wait here a minute with the baby. Just let me scope out the area, make sure it's Pat, and check that no one's got him under surveillance."

She frowned and looked around, snuggled the baby closer, and nodded.

With one deep breath to convince himself they'd be safe for a moment or two, he stood and inched forward, scanning the deserted street as he did. When he emerged from the tree line, the Jeep's passenger side door opened, and Pat climbed out.

Since the Jeep's brake lights remained lit, Adam assumed Jack had remained behind the wheel with his foot on the brake, ready to peel out of there the instant anything appeared off.

Pat jogged toward Adam, his gaze darting continuously up and down the street. When he reached him, he held out a hand. "Jaelyn?"

"Safe." Adam gestured for her to come forward even as he shook Pat's hand. "Thank you for coming, man."

"No problem. We have a safe house set up for all of you." He nodded, kissed Jaelyn's cheek when she emerged from the woods, and ran a finger over Leigha's cheek as he assessed her condition. Then he grinned. "This time, we didn't rent it in my name."

"Good choice." Adam laughed, and for the first time since they'd left the hospital, he felt like they might actually get a few hours of rest before they reassessed the situation and figured out how to move forward from there. As much as he was loath to admit it, he needed that time. Needed to rest, to catch his wind, to figure out his next move.

They headed toward the car, and as Adam opened the back door, he held his breath and scanned the area again.

Jaelyn slid in with the baby in her arms, and Pat shut the door behind her.

By the time Adam rounded the vehicle and hopped into the back seat behind Jack, Jaelyn already had the baby buckled into a car seat. "You're sure you weren't—"

A big, black dog leaned his head over the back seat from the cargo area and nudged Jaelyn's shoulder.

She laughed and wove her fingers into the thick fur around his neck. "Well, hello there, Shadow."

"Who does this handsome fellow belong to?" Adam petted the Bernese mountain dog, a beautiful animal with an equally incredible temperament if his behavior with Jaelyn was any indication.

Pat turned in his seat as Jack pulled away from the curb. "That's Shadow. He's my search and rescue dog, works with me at Seaport Fire and Rescue. Since the landline you called from came up private and I couldn't get back in touch with the two of you, I figured it best to bring him in case you had to take off before we could meet you at the rendezvous point."

Shadow rested his head on the seat back beside Jaelyn, and she leaned into him and closed her eyes. The woman had to be exhausted. She'd said she'd been working since seven the morning before, so it had been more than twenty-four hours since she'd slept. She needed rest. They all did.

"Which reminds me…" Pat held two cell phones out to Adam, along with a charger. "You said yours was damaged and Jaelyn's is gone, so at least these give you a way to reach out if you need help."

Adam nodded, touched by the amount of help these men were willing to offer, not only to Jaelyn, who was their friend, but to him, a complete stranger. "Thank you."

"No problem, man."

Adam looked down at Leigha, brushed a finger along

her cheek. She was so soft, so delicate, so fragile—how would they ever keep her safe? As much as Jaelyn needed rest, he was going to have to disturb her because, unfortunately, they needed a plan more.

"I'm not asleep." Jaelyn stared at him, her eyes clear, fingers absently stroking the dog's fur.

He smiled at her. "How'd you know I was about to wake you?"

"You think really loud." She grinned back at him, and the barrier he'd erected around his heart cracked just a little.

Seemed Leigha wasn't the only one sneaking past his defenses. Flustered, he ignored emotions he was far from ready to deal with and pushed on. "We have to rest for a few hours, and then we have to figure out what we're going to do."

"Jack and I have a suggestion…regarding the baby…" Pat shifted so he could study Adam. Since Jaelyn was directly behind him, he couldn't see her. So he missed the subtle stiffening of her posture, the hardening of her expression. "Jack and Ava offered to take her for a while, keep her until you get some of this sorted out."

A vise gripped Adam's heart, squeezed.

"No." Jaelyn's gaze shot to Adam, captured his and held. "I want to keep Leigha with me. For now, at least."

He wanted to protest, wanted to remind her they had killers on their heels, wanted to beg her to see reason, to turn the baby over to someone more able to look after her, and instead, he said nothing. He simply sat, staring at the child who'd somehow become so important to him that he didn't want to give her up, even for a little while.

He tore his gaze away from Leigha, forced himself to look out the window, commit their path to memory in case they once again had to flee, anything other than look upon an infant who should have no importance in his life other than to see she wasn't killed. And the best way to do that would be to let Jack and his wife take her.

And still he remained silent. He didn't want to disappoint Jaelyn, didn't want to hurt her by asking her to surrender the child.

*Liar.*

Bad enough he'd lied to Hank and Martha, who'd been nothing but open and kind to them, but now he was lying to himself as well. He opened his mouth to speak, to say all the things he knew in his mind he should say, yet he couldn't get the words past the lump clogging his throat.

He cleared his throat and turned his attention to the conversation still going on around him. Though it seemed he'd missed some of it, he caught the gist quickly enough—Jack and Pat would drop them off at the safe house. There was a car they could use in the garage, but the house wasn't stocked. Firefighters from Seaport Fire and Rescue would take turns on stakeout duty, while their police officer friend and a detective they knew quietly looked into who was coming after them. Though Adam suspected they'd never find a trace of anything to connect the men who'd come after Maya in the hospital and the B&B to the man pulling their strings or his hired hitman.

But he wasn't about to sit there and discuss that with a group of strangers. "How's Maya doing?"

Jack eyed him in the rearview mirror. "Her prognosis is good."

"Is she awake yet?"

"No, not yet, but they're hoping soon."

"Okay, that's good." Because he needed to ask her some questions, needed to determine if she'd be willing to turn over any evidence she might have and testify as to the identity of the Hunter.

His gaze shot once more to Leigha.

Or he could just let her go, allow her to disappear with her child and find peace instead of ending up like Josiah.

By the time Jack pulled up in front of a small, inline ranch house, Adam was on the verge of a full-on migraine. He got out of the car, breathed in the salty scent of the nearby bay. Blackness encroached, tunneling his vision, and he closed his eyes for just a moment, closed out everything…everyone.

"You okay?"

When he opened his eyes, Jaelyn stood face-to-face with him, concern marring her features. She lay a hand against his cheek as she had before, in a way that made him want to lean into her touch, take whatever comfort she offered.

"I'm okay. Just a bit stressed. Nothing a hot shower, a few hours of downtime…" *And confessing the truth about who Josiah Cameron was charged with killing* "…won't take care of."

He forced a smile and stepped back from her touch.

She let her hand drop to her side. Although she studied him for another moment, she made no further attempts to reach out.

His disappointment at that fact only served to annoy him. "We shouldn't be standing out in the open. Why don't you get Leigha inside while I do a quick perimeter check?"

She nodded, but if the grim look in her eyes was any indication, she probably suspected his perimeter check was only half about security and more to get alone time. And she'd be right about that. But, instead of being honest, he took the coward's way out and turned his back on her.

As he strolled along the sidewalk with his hands in his pockets, a deceptively casual pose to the unaware observer, he surveyed every house, road, alleyway, yard, vehicle, even the sky above them for any sign of possible surveillance. He found nothing but a middle-class neighborhood on a quiet Christmas morning, like a thousand other such neighborhoods dotting Long Island. He had to admit, Seaport was a charming little town where residents probably spent their weekends attending community fairs and church picnics. Undoubtedly, a wonderful place to raise a family.

He stopped short. What on earth was he thinking? He didn't have a family. They'd been taken from him in the most vicious attack. He was too overtired, couldn't focus, didn't have his head in the game. And that was dangerous. For everyone.

With a renewed sense of determination, he stopped procrastinating and strode up the walkway, waved to Pat and Jack, who sat across the street in the Jeep to keep an eye on things, and walked into the house.

Jaelyn had already curled into the corner of the couch

with the baby in her arms, feeding her a bottle and humming softly.

As much as he hated to intrude, it was time. Unfortunately, the memories this conversation would conjure would be painful for him to deal with, but there was no choice. Not for him. But for Jaelyn, well, there were other things she didn't need to know just yet, things that would only hurt her once she did. And, as he watched her brush the baby's cheek softly with a finger, he knew he'd be keeping those things to himself. For now, anyway.

He sat on the ottoman, facing her, leaned forward and rested his elbows on his knees. He clasped his hands together and met her gaze. "We need to talk."

She nodded and shifted the baby, giving him her full attention.

Leigha's gaze shifted as well, and he squirmed beneath both sets of dazzling blue eyes.

"Isn't she too young to pay attention like that?"

When Jaelyn smiled, a full-on genuine smile, it was as if she shook off the weight of the world. "She's not really paying attention to anything, just reacting to the sound of your voice, but she is very alert."

Adam smiled at the little bundle. He couldn't help himself. The child was going to be a beauty, with dark hair and brilliant blue eyes. Just like her mother—and like Jaelyn. He lifted his gaze to hers. A dull ache began in his chest, squeezed his heart. "I need to tell you about my wife."

"Your wife…the one you lost?"

"Yes. Alessandra was killed five years ago, along

with my unborn child, in retaliation for my allegations of corruption against…" *Your father.* The words almost slipped out, but he caught himself. No need to burden her with that truth just yet. There'd be plenty of time to hurt her with that one later on. "Senator Mark Lowell."

Tears sprang up in her eyes. She shifted Leigha so she could scoot forward and lay a hand over his. "I'm so sorry, Adam. I can't imagine the pain you must have gone through, must still be going through."

"No." He lowered his gaze to their hands, had to if he was going to get through telling this story without falling apart. "No, you can't. No one can, I guess, unless you've suffered that kind of loss."

She squeezed his hand, a gesture of support when there were no words that would bring comfort.

He blew out a breath. He supposed the worst of it was behind him, the admission his wife and child were gone because of him. Now there only remained the facts. "The witness who was killed, the one who was going to turn on the hitman in exchange for immunity from prosecution, was charged with Alessandra's murder."

# EIGHT

"You were defending your wife's killer?" The instant Jaelyn blurted out the words, she wished she could take them back. She cringed. "Sorry, I didn't mean—it just caught me off guard. Clearly, you believed he was innocent, and you've already said as much. I was just surprised, is all, that you'd have given him the chance to explain."

"No, it's okay. And you're right." Adam rested his elbows on his knees, lowered his face into his hands, and paused. He stayed that way for a moment, and Jaelyn was afraid he'd changed his mind about confiding in her, not that she would blame him after she'd shoved her foot so insensitively into her mouth.

"No, I'm not right. And I am truly sorry, sorry for what I said, and so very sorry about your wife and child." Losing her parents had left an emptiness in her heart. Turning to the man who was supposed to love her and finding out he'd been unfaithful had filled some of those empty places with bitterness, with a hardness that had kept her from feeling anything for anyone else, from allowing anyone to get too close. That had been the most difficult time in her life, and she'd built a shell around her heart to keep from ever suffering that kind of pain again.

But what Adam had gone through, losing his wife, his unborn child, and obviously shouldering a tremendous amount of guilt for what had happened…well… what would something like that do to a man? And yet, here he was, risking everything to save Maya and her child and Jaelyn. She wanted to reach out to him again, offer comfort, support, even just a shoulder to cry on, but she resisted the urge. She'd give him a few minutes, let him have the space he so clearly needed.

Then he stood, raked a hand through his hair, and crossed the room without saying anything.

"Well, I certainly blew that one." Jaelyn looked down into Leigha's eyes. "I think he needs a moment to himself."

The infant looked up at her, then gripped her finger and smiled.

A flood of joy flowed through Jaelyn. Though she'd cared for the child, protected her, connected with her on some basic level, this was the first time she'd just taken a moment to revel in the sheer delight of her. "You are so precious, little one."

Leigha cooed, waved her pudgy fist, taking Jaelyn's finger back and forth with her.

Jaelyn laughed, and for just an instant the weight of the world receded until there was nothing left but the two of them.

And then Adam returned to her and lay Maya's briefcase on the oversize ottoman, a stark reminder of the mess they'd gotten themselves into.

When Adam opened the lid, a tidal wave of anxiety crashed back over her. She wished so badly she'd met him under other circumstances, any other circumstances. She worked to steady her breathing, clutched the baby closer as Adam took a folder out of the briefcase.

"See this? Josiah Cameron was supposed to turn over the Hunter's hit list to me. He said it was coded but easy enough to understand if you knew what it was." He seemed to have reinforced whatever wall he'd erected to protect himself from the pain of the past. Adam held out an open folder and pointed to Senator Mark Lowell's name. He ran his finger across a line of numbers and letters, stopping at each to let her know what they meant. "I believe the good senator paid Hack Hunters the sum of two-million dollars to eliminate my wife, Alessandra Spencer, on this date five years ago. The same date my wife was shot and killed."

Jaelyn studied the information, tried to draw the same conclusion Adam had from the row of numbers and letters following the senator's name. While she couldn't deny the fact that it was possible he was reading the information accurately, she also couldn't help thinking the data could also mean something else. She had no idea what it meant, but it could be anything. She skimmed farther down the list, tried to make sense of the orderly lines of numbers and letters. There was no denying the date, the senator's name, even the dollar amount, but AS didn't have to be someone's initials. Sure, it was a mighty big coincidence the date happened to be the date Alessandra was shot. But still, there was no proof Maya had been carrying evidence her husband had killed anyone. And yet...

Could it be possible? Did Maya know her husband was a killer? Was she planning to turn the evidence over to the authorities? Or maybe blackmail him with it, exchange her silence for the lives of herself and her child? She needed to talk to Maya, needed answers that only she could give.

And then her gaze skimmed a few lines down and fell on another date from five years ago, followed by a set of initials. A chill raced through her, raising goose bumps. She lay a shaky finger on the line. "Here. This is the date of my parents' accident followed by the amount of three-million dollars and the initials DER plus one. Dr. Elijah Reed plus one." The chances of two coincidences lining up so perfectly, with dates and initials that matched *three* deaths that they knew of, were slim to none. "My mother didn't even rate her own initials, just plus one—an afterthought. And if he charges two-million dollars a hit, as it seems from the other numbers, my mother was not even worth the full amount."

"Jaelyn, I—"

She surged to her feet, dropped the folder, scattering the pages across the floor, and shifted the baby into Adam's arms. She ignored his shocked sputtering and bolted for the door. Better to take her chances a killer was lying in wait somewhere out there than to sit in this room with the claustrophobia threatening to suffocate her for even another second. She yanked the front door open and strode out onto the front lawn.

But where could she go? There was nowhere to run, nowhere to hide, nowhere she'd be safe, nowhere she could escape from the certainty that not only was Adam right about having found a copy of the Hunter's hit list in Maya's possession, but that her own parents had not died accidentally. They had been deliberately murdered.

She bent, propped her hands on her knees, and sucked in deep lungsful of the cold, damp air. The ache in her chest begged for relief. She coughed, as sobs began to rack her body.

How could that be? They had to be reading the list wrong. Why would Maya's husband or the senator have had any reason to kill Jaelyn's parents? Everyone loved them. Elijah and Allison Reed were outstanding members of the community. Her mother had volunteered at the church, the hospital, the PTA, and anywhere else she was needed.

And then Adam was beside her. He rested a hand on her back, circling her arm with his other hand. "Come on now, Jaelyn. It's not safe out here."

"Where's Leigha?"

"I buckled her into the seat. I didn't want to bring her out here and expose her to whoever might be watching." Adam lifted a hand, waved to whichever firefighter had drawn the short straw and was spending Christmas Day on stakeout duty to let him know everything was okay.

But it wasn't okay, and it might never be okay. Her gaze shot to his, and she searched his expression for answers, for hope, for something…anything…that would help her understand what was happening to her and why. "I don't understand what's going on, why my entire world has just been turned completely upside down."

"I know." He rubbed a circle on her back, guided her toward the house, ignored everything else that might be happening around them to keep his attention firmly on her. "And I promise you we're going to figure it out. I'm sorry this is all happening, sorry you didn't know any of it before now."

She appreciated that, but it didn't ease the pain or uncertainty, didn't change the fact that her entire life— even her parents' deaths—had been a lie.

"Hey." He lay a finger gently beneath her chin, tipped her face toward him. "Listen to me. I promise you we'll get to the bottom of this. I will not rest until I have the answers you need."

She nodded and let him lead her inside, settle her on the couch. Since Leigha had fallen asleep, she left her in the seat and felt the baby's absence from her arms more painfully than she was willing to admit, even to herself.

Adam sat on the ottoman facing her, gripped her hands in his. "Are you okay now?"

Was she? Actually, she had no idea. A short burst of laughter blurted out.

Adam simply stared at her for a moment and lifted a brow, then he grinned, the gold flecks amid the browns and greens in his eyes dancing with humor.

She shook her head and sighed. "We're a hot mess."

"Ah, well…" He laughed then, and relaxed, the stiffness in his posture easing. "I can't really argue that, but I can't think of anyone else I'd rather be in this mess with."

Jaelyn studied him as he frowned, seeming confused that he'd allowed the sentiment to slip out. Then she squeezed his hands. "No, me neither."

And that was true. It had been so long since she'd allowed anyone to penetrate the shell she'd created. She didn't count her friends and coworkers, because that was different. This, though—whatever this was between her and Adam—well, she was beginning to think God had completely upended her life and then thrown Adam into her path to test her. And so far, she was failing miserably. Although, they *were* still alive, and Leigha was safe—she slid a finger into the baby's tiny fist—so maybe she hadn't completely botched it.

Adam fidgeted with her fingers, cradling her hand in both of his. "Okay, I think we've both dealt as best we can with the most difficult emotional parts of all this. Now we have to lay it all out and come up with some sort of a logical plan."

She nodded. The rest could be dealt with later, when they were safe. She'd definitely need some time to reassess her priorities, determine where she wanted her life to go from here, but now wasn't the time. "Fine, so let's go over what we know and figure out what to do next."

He released her hand, pulled back to sit up straighter. She told herself the disappointment was only because she felt safer with him near, then immediately dismissed the thought.

"Okay. Josiah Cameron was not only Maya's lover but Senator Lowell's most trusted aide. In addition to pointing the finger at the Hunter, he was also set to testify that the senator himself had hired the hitman to commit the murder Josiah was arrested for, the murder of my wife, which Josiah was then framed for."

"But why frame Josiah?"

Adam shrugged. "Who knows? Maybe Hunter Barlowe figured out Josiah was having an affair with his wife. He could have seen Josiah sentenced to prison for the rest of his life, then waited a while and done away with Maya. Or maybe it was his way of punishing Maya, as the senator punished me by killing my wife."

"Or…" Jaelyn reviewed the timeline in her head. "How long were Maya and Josiah having an affair?"

"Years."

"And Leigha? Presumably Josiah is her father?"

He spread his hands wide, shook his head. "I can only assume so, since I didn't know of her existence before last night."

"Hmm…" She chewed it over. "Maybe Hunter found out his wife was pregnant and the child wasn't his? He could easily have gotten rid of Josiah by framing him, throwing suspicion off the senator after you'd accused him of being corrupt. That would eliminate Josiah as a problem. Plus, even if Josiah did point a finger at Hunter Barlowe, even if he did accuse him of being a hitman, even if he could come up with some kind of proof, like the documents we have here, who'd believe him? Hunter could say Josiah was lying to get him out of the picture so he could have Maya, or that Maya and Josiah planted the evidence pointing down a trail toward her husband as a gun for hire."

"I suppose any of that is possible."

"You know for sure Lowell is corrupt?"

He scoffed. "That man is as low as they come. He uses bribery, blackmail, intimidation, anything to get his way. He uses women one after another then pays them off to keep their mouths shut. Those who won't accept payment in return for silence disappear."

"And you have proof of this?"

"No, not really, just a long list of people—including a junior partner at my firm who was accosted by the senator then tossed aside—who knew exactly what kind of monster that man is. Of course, when it came time for any of them to come forward and testify before a grand jury, to put up or shut up, Alessandra was killed." He scrubbed a hand down his face. "Maybe to punish me, maybe to distract me, maybe as a warning to those set to testify. Either way, suddenly, all of my witnesses had a mass amnesia attack. Even the junior partner. She cried uncontrollably when she told me she couldn't remember anything and wouldn't be testifying. Of course, I understood. How could I not? She had family too."

She reached out to him, wove her fingers through his. "We'll stop him, Adam. We'll get justice for Alessandra and your child. I'm sorry it couldn't be more, sorry it's coming too late to save them."

He nodded, kept his gaze locked on their intertwined fingers. "I'm sorry about your parents, Jaelyn. That they were killed, and sorry they didn't live long enough to explain the truth to you."

"Yeah. Me too." An ache throbbed deep inside her heart, where she could do nothing to alleviate the pain.

"But I have to think that they had their reasons for keeping quiet." He tilted her chin up to catch her gaze and hold it captive. "The child they raised is a beautiful person, one who risked her own life without hesitation to save a stranger. One who has dedicated herself to helping others, both as an ER nurse and a firefighter, and one who took in a stranger's child amid all of this confusion and tended to her with love and affection. It seems to me they would have been close with their daughter, honest with her at all costs."

"And until yesterday I'd have sworn that was true." Would have believed it with every last ounce of her being.

"Then trust them."

She frowned. "What do you mean?"

"Trust that if they didn't tell you about the adoption there was a reason for that. If they didn't tell you about Maya, maybe they didn't know about her. I've asked my paralegal to look into the situation and see what she can find out."

Jaelyn only nodded. As much as she wanted answers about the adoption, they needed to focus on the situation at hand first. Too many lives were at stake for her to indulge in a personal campaign.

"When did you take the DNA test? And when did you find out about Maya?"

"I took the DNA test last winter. There was a blizzard and the guys were sitting around the firehouse, bored, and had a bunch of DNA tests they were all taking. They asked me if I wanted to do one too, so I did. Why not, right? A look into my past, a way to see where my family came from…an attempt to feel close to them once more even though they were gone." And for that one fleeting moment, she'd been able to hold onto them again. But instead of bringing her family back to her, the knowledge of her past had driven a wedge between them.

He nodded for her to continue.

"Then the results came back telling me where I was from but not much else. But then there was a friends and family app you could join to connect you to long lost family members. I figured maybe there was an odd cousin or other distant relative I'd never heard of."

"And Maya's name came up?"

"No." She remembered that clearly, no one else had come up and she'd been slightly disappointed, hadn't even realized she was hoping for some family connection to ease some of the loss. "It wasn't until a month ago that Maya's name popped up."

"But you didn't reach out to her?"

"No, I was too confused. If it had been a cousin, an aunt or uncle, I'd have reached out, but a sister? A twin, no less? At first I thought it was a mistake or something, but then I just set it aside to stew for a while and hadn't decided what to do about it yet when Maya was brought into the ER."

"Okay, but she knew about you—had to have, if she was going to forge all those documents. She had to have known months ago if Leigha's birth certificate is to be believed."

Jaelyn nodded slowly. "Or she forged that within the past few weeks as well, along with all the other documents."

Adam held the cell phone Pat had given him out to

her. "Can you access the app on here? I'm curious if it will tell you when Maya's information was added to the site."

"Okay." She took the phone to log in. She didn't remember any notice of when Maya had first shown up in the app, but honestly, she'd been so blindsided by the whole thing, she hadn't bothered to look. An error message popped up. "Hmm…it says my account doesn't exist."

"Did you enter the right username and password?"

Irritated, she shot him a glare. She might not be a computer whiz, but she could enter a username and password. She re-entered the information, careful not to hit the wrong buttons while she typed. "Still no account registered with these credentials."

"Can you search for Maya's name? See if her profile is there?"

She tried it. "It won't let me access that information without an account."

"All right, don't worry about it."

Why would her account suddenly be inaccessible? "Do you think Maya deleted my account so no one would find me?"

"It's possible. She'd certainly have the knowledge and ability to do so."

*But why?* The question hung heavy in the air between them.

Jaelyn rested her elbows on her knees, lowered her face into her hands. A stress headache beat at her.

Adam folded his arms across his knees, leaned forward until his forehead pressed against hers. "We're not going to find answers to any of that, not yet anyway, probably not until Maya is released from the hospital and can answer questions herself."

"So what do we do now?"

He frowned. "Well, the way I see it, all we've been doing is reacting."

And too emotionally, at that. He was right. They needed to set all feelings aside and develop a logical plan.

"We need to move ahead with what we can do something about," Adam said. "Getting the senator's goons to come after us again. We draw them out, this time with the police waiting to apprehend and question them, and get some answers that way."

Although Jaelyn seemed surprised her account was missing, Adam wasn't. Whether Maya knew about her husband's career choice or not, she was a cybersecurity expert. Hacking Jaelyn's account and deleting it along with her own would have been child's play. And he was beginning to think Maya had a plan in mind all along, one that didn't include leaving hers or Jaelyn's DNA lying around for anyone to find.

If she'd known she had a twin, she might have been searching for her. Without knowing the circumstances of Jaelyn's adoption, it was possible she hadn't been able to find her twin no matter what mad cyber skills she possessed.

Either way, that was a problem for another time. Right now, he had to decide whether to tell Jaelyn the very killer who'd ordered the hits on the parents she remembered, the ones she'd been so close with, the ones who'd raised her to be the warm, caring, incredible person she'd become, was actually her biological father.

He thought back to the punch of shock he'd felt when Josiah Cameron had first walked through his office door.

Adam hadn't known the whole story at that time, only that the senator's aide had been arrested for Alessandra's murder five years after the fact. Since Josiah had such a close connection to the man Adam knew had orchestrated the murder, he'd had no reason to doubt that Josiah was the killer he'd been searching for. He'd been so sure about it that the first thing he'd done when Josiah walked into his office requesting his help was punch him square in the jaw, knocking him out cold.

He rubbed his knuckles, sore at the memory.

But after Josiah had regained consciousness, he'd begged Adam to listen. Adam had listened, and he'd believed. Every word. There would be plenty of time to tell Jaelyn about her real father. For now, he'd let her struggle with the memory of the only parents she'd ever known, with the betrayal she was battling, with the sister Adam wasn't sure had her best interests at heart.

Maya might have put Jaelyn's name on the baby's birth certificate to hide her from the senator or Hunter. She may have been determined to continue where Josiah left off and turn over the evidence in her possession that the Hunter was Senator Lowell's hired gun. In which case, Maya was ready to sacrifice herself to protect her child and a sister she didn't even know. Could the woman possibly be that selfless?

He glanced at Jaelyn, studied her as she looked down

at the sleeping baby, rubbing her thumb back and forth over the hand gripping her finger. Yes, maybe she was. Maybe the two shared the same selfless traits. If so, they must have gotten it from their mother.

Because if Maya was anything like her biological father, it was more likely she forged documents in Jaelyn's name so she could assume Jaelyn's identity and go on the run with the baby herself.

Jaelyn cleared her throat, interrupting his thoughts and saving him from contemplating further.

"I had an idea."

"Okay." But he was still distracted, his thoughts ricocheting scattershot around his skull.

"I think I might know a way to get the hitmen to come after me."

A ball of dread curdled in his gut. While he wanted the men to come after him, couldn't think of any other way to get the answers they so desperately needed, the thought of them anywhere near Jaelyn or Leigha turned his stomach.

At the same time, these were the men responsible for Alessandra's death, for their child's death. Didn't he owe it to them to use any and all means at his disposal to bring their killers to justice? "How?"

"When I was going through Maya's briefcase, I noticed she's on the same thyroid medication as I am."

That didn't surprise him, considering they were twins.

"I lost mine when I lost my bag, and I took one of Maya's this morning so I wouldn't miss a dose." She looked at him. "So, I was thinking, what if I call a local pharmacy and pretend to be Maya, tell them I lost my medication."

Adam scooted closer. She might be onto something. "They'd have to submit it through the insurance company."

Jaelyn nodded. "I mean, Maya could pay cash for it, but either way, the pharmacy would have to get the prescription from the doctor, even if they didn't get approval from the insurance company. If the senator has connections, or if Hunter Barlowe is a cybersecurity expert, surely they'd be monitoring any and all of Maya's accounts."

His body rocked in rhythm with the pounding in his head, bringing a sudden wave of queasiness. Motion sickness, nothing more, and nothing at all to do with the fact that Jaelyn wanted to set herself up to be used as bait. After all, hadn't they done the same at the B&B? But that had been before he'd gotten to know her. "Maybe."

"I figured, since she used a midwife to deliver Leigha, she might expect her husband or the senator to be monitoring her doctor's calls as well, or hacking his records. Is that possible?"

"Hmm…" He played it out in his mind. It was possible, he supposed. And they had nothing to lose by trying. "It's a good idea, and it might work, but I think we can tweak the odds in our favor."

"Oh? How's that?"

"Get in touch with Pat. Find out if Maya had a cell phone in her possession when she was brought in. It wasn't in her bag or we'd have found it, so maybe it was on her person. It's a long shot, considering Maya most likely wouldn't have been using her own phone, but it wouldn't hurt to ask. If we can get that phone, and you can make the call from it—"

"You think they've got her cell phone tapped?"

"I don't know, but it's possible, and if nothing else, it gives them one more way to track her. So, we use her phone, call her doctor's office... Is the pharmacy a chain?"

Leigha let out a loud cry, startling him. When Jaelyn reached for her, he lay a hand on her arm. "I'll get her this time."

She arched a brow but said nothing, simply prepared a bottle while he lifted Leigha from the seat and cradled her in his arms.

He held her gently, afraid he might inadvertently hurt her. "She seems delicate enough to break."

"Don't worry, she's not that fragile." Jaelyn handed him the bottle then leaned over Leigha. "Are you? I think you're stronger than any of us know."

*Just like her aunt.* The thought brought a flare of heat to his cheeks, along with a wave of gratitude that he'd managed to keep from saying it out loud. He rubbed the tip of the bottle against Leigha's lips as he'd seen Jaelyn do, and she opened her mouth and started to drink.

"Where were we? Oh, right, the pharmacy." Jaelyn returned to her seat. "Yes. The name was on the label, and there's one nearby."

"So we have the prescription called in to them and try to put it through her insurance. Even if they decline it because it's too soon to renew, anyone monitoring would pick it up."

"And then?"

Some of the churning in his gut had begun to turn to anticipation. "Then, you have them charge it to whatever card she has on file. I have no doubt they'll pick up on that."

"But would Maya make a mistake like that?"

"Who's to say it's her mistake?" He grinned, finally seeing an end in sight. If they could pull this off... "Maybe the pharmacy just ran the card on file like usual. It doesn't matter if it's likely, only that whoever might be watching believes it could be plausible. Either way, if her credit card gets used, they'd have no choice but to follow up."

"And then what?" She tilted her head, studied him in that quietly observant way she had. "Do we go to the pharmacy? Hope they show up?"

"No." She wasn't going to like this part, but he'd have to convince her, because there were no other options. He wouldn't get justice for his wife and child at the expense of an innocent woman. "I talk to Pat and Jack, and they can get in touch with your friend, the police officer..."

"Gabe," she supplied.

"Yes, Gabe. And the police can net anyone they find lingering outside the pharmacy."

She was already shaking her head. "It's not going to work. They'll be waiting for me, I mean Maya, to show up. Chances are they won't make a move until she does. The police can't arrest them for hanging around outside a pharmacy. They have to actually do something first."

She was right, though he was loath to admit it. "Okay, all right, we'll figure it out. In the meantime, we have to find out if the gunman from the hospital ever regained consciousness."

"He hadn't the last time I spoke to Pat to check on Maya." She frowned. "Neither had Maya."

"Okay. All right." His thoughts raced. "I'd like to talk to Gabe, see what he thinks. Are you okay with that?"

"Yes, I'll set up a meet."

"Don't have him come here. I'll go out and meet him somewhere else, anywhere that's convenient." The fewer people they had coming to the safe house the better, since they had no way to know who might be followed. He looked down at the baby still drinking the bottle in his arms and found her staring back at him with those innocent blue eyes filled with wonder. Besides, he needed a breather, some space away from Jaelyn and the baby he was starting to grow too attached to. He had to clear his head of them if he was going to think straight.

She nodded absently as she lifted the phone and made the call.

They had a little time, anyway. Since it was afternoon on Christmas Day, the pharmacy and the doctor's office would be closed. The soonest they could move would be the next day, which gave him plenty of time to go over the plan with Gabe and make sure Jaelyn's safety was a priority.

"Pat said they can meet with you now in the diner parking lot in town."

Her voice startled him. "Huh? Oh, right."

"Do me a favor?" With her attention on the baby, she didn't seem to notice his distractedness.

"What's that?"

"Pick up diapers on your way back if you can find anywhere open."

He laughed at the mundane request, as if they weren't in the midst of contemplating a life-and-death situation. "Yes, dear."

Her gaze shot to his, humor lighting her eyes. "Thanks, hon."

He sobered almost immediately, then stood, set the bottle aside and reluctantly handed Leigha over to her. "Make sure you stay inside and keep the doors locked. I'll stop by and check with whoever's on stakeout duty out there and let them know I'm leaving."

She nodded. "Sure."

"Hey." He met her gaze, willed her to know he considered her safety a priority, though he couldn't bring himself to make the admission out loud. It felt like too much of a betrayal to the wife he'd lost only because of her loyalty to him. "Are you sure you're okay with me leaving? If not, we can work something else out."

The thought of that brought a little too much relief.

"No, it's okay, I'm fine. It's safer for Leigha if I stay here with her." She searched his gaze, looked deep into his eyes, and seemed satisfied with whatever she found there. "Just be careful."

"I will." He pushed a few strands of loose hair behind her ear, gave a little tug. "I'll be back in no time."

She smiled, lay her hand over his where he still held her hair, and leaned her cheek into his palm for just a moment. Tears shimmered in her eyes but didn't fall, and then she stepped back and looked away.

Adam turned and walked out before he could change his mind. After stopping to speak to two of Jaelyn's friends, volunteer firefighters from Seaport, he jumped in the SUV Pat and Jack had mentioned was in the garage, turned on the ignition, then just sat there. Were they really safer there alone then they'd be with him?

There was a high possibility Seaport Fire and Rescue would be under surveillance and someone could follow Pat when he left, since they'd already connected him to her. Taking Jaelyn anywhere would be dangerous for everyone involved. And yet…the thought of leaving her alone sat like a brick in his gut. His growing feelings for her—

He had no feelings for her, growing or otherwise. His only thought was to keep the woman and infant safe and get justice for his wife and child. Beyond that… well, there was no beyond that. He'd resume his life in New York City, return to his role as a defense attorney, though the thought didn't bring as much satisfaction as it once had. He might be able to return to defending those who were falsely accused, but what of those who weren't? Did he really want to spend his life getting criminals a free ride? But then some people, like Josiah Cameron, were innocent and deserved justice. Weren't those the ones he'd wanted to save and the reason he became a defense attorney in the first place?

He shook off the thoughts. There would be plenty of time to contemplate whatever path his life would take after he saw Senator Lowell and Hunter Barlowe behind bars. And right now, it was time to take the first step toward accomplishing that goal.

# NINE

Jaelyn paced the confines of the small living room feeling caged. She bounced and rocked Leigha, who'd been crying for the better part of an hour, as she strode back and forth, her back on fire. "Shh…baby. Shh. It's okay."

She hummed softly, hoping to soothe, but nothing worked. She'd fed her, changed her, rocked her, sang to her. Nothing she did consoled the poor child.

Added to her concern for Leigha, Adam still hadn't called or returned. He'd been gone for hours. Surely, they had to have worked something out by now. What if he'd taken off, given up on her and Leigha and gone after the senator on his own? Would he betray her that way? Maybe, but she didn't think so. And even if he had, she was dead certain it would only have been for her and Leigha's protection.

She warred with herself over calling Pat, then vetoed the idea. What if they were somewhere he could be overheard? Besides, it felt like a betrayal, as if she didn't trust Adam. She'd thought of going outside and asking whoever was on stakeout if they could check in, but that didn't seem any better.

She paused to massage her throbbing back, told herself she was simply concerned for Adam's safety, nothing more than that. But was that true? Because somewhere along the line, she feared she'd begun to develop something for Adam that she hadn't been able to feel for five long years…trust. And the thought scared her nearly as much as the killers on their heels.

Leigha let out one long wail, stiffened her body, and threw herself back.

Jaelyn fumbled at the unexpected move but caught the back of her head. "It's okay, little one."

The baby's face turned bright red as she continued to wail.

"Okay, sweetie, let's try something else." Because Jaelyn needed to sit for a minute, ease the ache in her back. She perched on the edge of the couch, lay Leigha on the ottoman where Adam had sat facing her only a few short hours earlier. She dug through the diaper bag and came up with a small stuffed giraffe and shook it gently. "How about this, huh? Do you like that?"

The cries tapered off for a moment, while Leigha seemed to study the rattling sound, then resumed.

"Oh, Leigha, I don't know what to do for you." She lifted the baby's legs, pushed them toward her stomach, eased back, then repeated the process. "There now, honey, don't cry."

The cries eased off to soft sobs and sniffles. Her eyes fluttered closed.

The front door opened, and it startled Jaelyn.

Leigha let out a long, loud cry.

Jaelyn turned to find Adam standing in the doorway, two bags clutched in his hands, frowning. "Is she okay?"

Jaelyn stood, lifted Leigha into her arms again, and held her close. She refused to acknowledge the relief pouring through her at his return. "I think so. At least, I can't find anything wrong, she just won't stop crying."

Adam set the bags on a small cabinet in the entryway and crossed to her. He studied the baby, ran a finger over her cheek. "It's okay, Leigha, I brought you a surprise."

Jaelyn glanced at him and lifted a brow. "I guess you found diapers?"

"No, well, I mean, yes. I did find a convenience store open and was able to get diapers, but that's not the surprise."

Leigha turned her head toward the sound of his voice. Fat tears shimmered on her bright red cheeks.

"I have to run out to the car for it." With that, he turned and fled.

Jaelyn couldn't help but laugh. He seemed so distraught. It was the first time she could recall seeing him so lacking in confidence. "Seems you bring out the softer side of our hero, doesn't it?"

She caught herself. Hero? Is that what Adam was to her? No, not really, but not so far off either. After all, had he not shown up at the emergency department when he did, Jaelyn would surely have been killed by the gunman and who knows what would have happened to Leigha.

She turned away from the thought, couldn't stand to think what might have happened to Leigha, and clutched her closer.

When Adam returned, he carried a small, scrawny

Christmas tree decorated with miniature coffee cups, an assortment of candy bar ornaments, and a few red and green balls.

Warmth radiated through Jaelyn. "Where in the world did you find that?"

"It was sitting on the counter in the convenience store, and I got to thinking, well…" He paused, set the bag down, then put the tree on a side table in the living room and plugged it in. The colorful lights flicked on. When Adam turned to her, with the lights from the tree washing over him in a rainbow of color, he grinned. "No matter what's going on right now, it is Leigha's first Christmas, and I thought she should get to celebrate."

With a lump in her throat she had no hope of swallowing down, Jaelyn simply nodded and shifted the baby to face the tree.

Tears shimmered in Leigha's eyes, darkening her lashes, but the sobs lessened as her gaze focused on the blinking lights. She waved her arms, bounced her legs, and babbled.

"Looks like she likes it." Adam smiled from ear to ear.

"Yes, that was a really thoughtful thing to do, Adam."

He shrugged it off. "It just struck me is all, when I was standing there in the store, scanning the lot for any potential threats, that today is a day that should be celebrated regardless of whatever else might be going on."

She reached for his hand, gripped it in hers. "Yes, you're right, it is."

"Besides, when I saw the tree, it stirred something in me, something I haven't felt in five years. Faith." He squeezed her hand. "For the first time in so long, I felt not only a return of faith, but of hope as well. As if maybe welcoming God back into my heart has eased some of the pain and grief I've lived with for so long."

She smiled softly. "I'd say God has answered more than one of our prayers in the past hours."

"Yes. Yes, He has." His gaze fell on Leigha as he brushed a hand over her hair, then turned to Jaelyn, his expression serious. "I have a gift for you too."

"For me?" Surprise ran through her, along with a sense of disorientation. Seemed Adam had a way of throwing her off balance.

"Yes, but for now, while Leigha seems mesmerized by the colorful lights, why don't we sit down and eat something?"

Leaving her to settle the baby, he returned to the entryway and grabbed the bags, then set them on the ottoman.

Jaelyn buckled Leigha into the borrowed seat and turned her to face the blinking lights.

The baby put one fist in her mouth, her attention riveted on the tree.

"Sorry, this is the best I could do." Adam unpacked premade sandwiches and soft drinks.

"Are you kidding me?" She lay a hand over her rumbling stomach. "This is perfect. I'm starved."

"Me too." He dragged an armchair across the room and set it beside the ottoman, then sat across from her, using the ottoman as a table. He handed her a sandwich. "Eat while I tell you what's going on."

She nodded and unwrapped the sandwich, trying to ignore the anticipation of whatever Adam was going to say. Was it news? Could they have found a way to stop Hunter Barlowe and Senator Lowell? She ate slowly while Adam outlined the plan for the next day between bites. Things would pretty much go as they'd planned, with Gabe and a detective he knew setting up to take whoever showed up to grab her into custody. The consensus was they'd still try to take Maya alive rather than kill her, since they seemed to want something from her.

Jaelyn struggled to pay attention to the logistics of the plan, while her mind betrayed her and ran through all the things that could possibly go wrong. What if they were ready to just eliminate Maya? What if they figured out it was Jaelyn and not Maya? Would they simply kill her? All the officers in the world surrounding her wouldn't stop a sniper shooting from a distance. Then again, Seaport sat close to sea level on a flat stretch of land. There were no high-rise buildings around for a sniper to settle in and wait for her to show up, and —

"…pick up Leigha."

The baby's name yanked her from her thoughts. "Wait. What?"

"Jack and Ava are going to pick up Leigha first thing in the morning, before you call the pharmacy and set the plan in motion." Done with his sandwich, Adam balled the paper wrapper and dropped it into one of the empty bags, then opened a bag of chips.

"Why are they picking her up so early?" Although she understood she couldn't take Leigha with her, the thought of handing her over to anyone else had the few bites of sandwich she'd managed weighing heavily and threatening to rebel.

"We have to be ready to move at a moment's notice."

She nodded, couldn't argue with his logic, but she didn't have to like it. With her appetite gone, she re-wrapped her sandwich and set it aside.

"You okay?"

"I am, yes." Surprisingly so, all things considered. At least now they had a plan in place and hopefully an ending to this whole mess in sight.

"Good, then." He cleaned up and set their garbage and the remainder of the food aside, then sat on the ottoman facing her, elbows resting on his knees, hands clasped together. "There's something else I want to tell you about, the gift of sorts I mentioned earlier."

She swiped her sweaty palms on her leggings, suddenly nervous. She checked on Leigha, who'd finally fallen asleep amid the glow of the Christmas lights.

"I didn't expect my paralegal to get to anything today, but apparently, she had some time this afternoon and made a few phone calls, rousted a few people from their holiday festivities."

"Wow, I'm surprised she went through the trouble on Christmas."

"Yeah, well, the junior partner I told you about is a good friend of hers. While Carrie wasn't able to talk her into testifying, she did say she'd drop anything anytime if I needed help with this case. Anyway…"

Jaelyn held her breath, waited.

"Eventually, she ended up speaking with a Dr. Vance Sajak…" He let the name hang between them, seemed to be waiting for some response.

"He was a good friend of my father's, worked with

him at the hospital." A good man Jaelyn remembered fondly, though he was often too busy to attend functions, and she hadn't seen him in years. He was one of the people Jaelyn had considered contacting when she'd found out the truth about Maya. If anyone would know about her adoption, it would be him.

And suddenly she wanted to beg Adam to stop, to keep whatever he'd learned to himself, because once he said it out loud, once she knew the truth, there would be no going back, no return to the safe little lie she'd lived most of her life.

"You and Maya were both put up for adoption by your birth mother as newborns," Adam relayed gently. "You were supposed to go to the same parents, but you were sick when you were born, and they didn't expect you to make it. The couple who adopted Maya, well…"

Was there a kind way to say they didn't feel like dealing with a sickly infant? Didn't want to risk getting attached and then losing a baby they'd paid good money for? The thought had been turning over like a ball of grease in his gut since he'd learned of it. "They weren't able to take on a newborn with the complications you had. So, they only took Maya."

"What?"

He almost stopped there at the hurt in her eyes, but the Reeds had been amazing people. And if the person she'd become, based on what little he knew about her, was a result of their upbringing, she'd gotten the better end of the deal. The story of her adoption was the one good thing he could give her. "The doctor who was taking care of you, Dr. Reed, fell in love with your strength, your courage, your tenacity, and he told his wife about you. She went to the hospital, sat beside you for hours on end, cradled you in her arms, and decided no child should be without a mother, no matter what the outcome would be. So he and his wife adopted you."

Tears shimmered in her gaze, deepening the blue of her eyes, darkening her thick lashes. They then tipped over and rolled down her cheeks. "Vance knew all of that?"

"He did, yes." He reached for her hands, found them shaking and cold. "And you recovered, grew strong with them at your side. As to why they never told you, Vance said that was part of the deal with your birth mother, that they'd raise you as their own, never tell anyone else the truth of it all. Since Vance was there at the time, he knew all of it. He said your father confided in him that your birth mother seemed frightened. He figured your father was abusive and she was trying to protect you from him."

Which was true enough. Mark Lowell was not only abusive but a killer—even if he'd only requested the hits. If the list they'd found in Maya's briefcase was what they suspected, he'd known about Jaelyn, about the couple who'd adopted her, so why did he wait so long to have them killed? Had he only just found out about her at that time? And what about Maya's adoptive parents? Had they been killed on his orders as well? He needed to look more closely into the couple who'd died in a freak boating accident just after Maya had turned nineteen.

Too many thoughts crowded his mind, all begging for attention, for answers he just didn't have.

"Thank you, Adam, for finding out what happened and for letting me know." She slid her hand from his, tucked her hair behind her ear, and stood. "I think I'm going to try to get some sleep now. Tomorrow promises to be a long day."

While that was true enough, he suspected her retreat had more to do with taking time to process all he'd told her than it did with trying to rest. But he let her go anyway, resisted the urge to pull her close, to hold her in his arms and promise everything would be okay. The last time he'd made that promise, it had turned out to be a lie. A lie that had haunted him for the last five years and surely always would.

She took Leigha with her into one of the bedrooms and closed the door softly, leaving Adam alone with his thoughts.

Unfortunately, they were not good company. He sat on the couch, propped his feet on the ottoman, and ran through the plan again. Jaelyn would make the necessary phone calls first thing in the morning, although, as he'd suspected, they didn't find a cell phone in Maya's pockets. When she arrived at the pharmacy, the police would already be in place, with undercover officers inside the pharmacy and others surrounding the parking lot.

If anyone came after Jaelyn when she arrived, they should be able to apprehend them. So why was his stomach in knots? What hadn't they anticipated that could go wrong?

That thought followed him into a restless sleep, chased

him through nightmares, and hounded him when the first rays of light peeked through the windows the next morning.

By the time a knock sounded on the door an hour later, he was as ready as he was going to get.

Jaelyn still hadn't emerged from the bedroom when he opened the door to Jack and Ava, whom he'd met at the diner when he'd gone to speak to Gabe. They were accompanied by a beautiful little girl with a mass of blonde curls and big blue eyes that held far more cunning than her age should allow.

Jack shook his proffered hand. "Adam, this is Missy."

Missy, who couldn't be older than four, held out a hand to him and smiled. "It's nice to meet you."

"It's nice to meet you too, Missy." He ushered them inside, scanned the quiet neighborhood, and shut the door. Everything in him wanted to tell them to leave, that he'd changed his mind, that he'd go on the run with Jaelyn and Leigha until they could come up with a better plan that didn't put either of them in the crosshairs of a killer.

Ava held out a cup carrier with two coffees and a plastic bag. "We figured you probably haven't had breakfast yet."

"No, we haven't. Thank you." Though he took the bag and cupholder from her, he doubted he'd be able to get anything down until after this was done. "Why don't you guys have a seat in the living room while I get Jaelyn and Leigha?"

He left them, headed for her bedroom door, and knocked softly. "Jaelyn?"

"Come in."

He opened the door, poked his head in, not sure what kind of mood to expect, then leaned against the doorjamb. She seemed okay, though dark circles ringed her eyes. He had no doubt she hadn't slept much. "Jack and Ava are here with Missy."

She smiled. "Isn't she a sweetheart?"

"She sure seems to be, but I'm reserving judgment. I've heard stories." He grinned, hoping to lighten her mood.

"I bet you have if you've hung out with Jack for more than a few minutes. Don't let those baby blues fool you. Missy is a handful and a half."

He laughed, happy she seemed okay.

She took one last look around the room, slung the diaper bag over her shoulder and handed him the journal and forged documents. "Can you put these in Maya's briefcase with the rest of the documents, please?"

"Sure thing." He took them from her and lay a hand against her arm when she started past him with Leigha, who was already bundled into her seat. "You trust Jack and Ava, right?"

She inhaled deeply, let out a slow, shaky breath. "I trust Jack with my life on a regular basis. But this, trusting him with Leigha, well...let's just say I find trusting anyone difficult. But if I have to trust someone, I guess Jack and Ava are about as loyal as they come."

He nodded, relieved and yet...he didn't want to let the baby out of his sight. He couldn't imagine what Jaelyn must be going through. Thoughts of what might happen in the future tortured him. Jaelyn had become too attached to the baby, especially considering they had no real understanding of the circumstances or what was going on with Maya. What if Maya took off with her after this was all done, and they never saw her or the baby again? How would Jaelyn handle that? If the shadows surrounding her red-rimmed eyes were any indication, she'd spent the night tossing and turning, probably contemplating something along those same lines.

He shoved the thoughts aside. They'd have to deal with whatever came later, when the time came. He kissed Jaelyn's temple. "Come on. Let's get this done."

She sniffed, nodded, and moved past him into the hallway.

Adam followed her into the living room.

The instant she walked in with the baby, Missy let out a delighted squeal. "Can I hold her?"

"Not right now, honey, but you can later on if you listen really well, okay?" Ava said.

"Uh huh." She clasped her hands together against her chest and bent over Leigha. "Hello, baby."

Leigha smiled.

Ava took the seat from Jaelyn, rubbed a hand up and down her arm. "I promise we'll take good care of her, Jaelyn. Missy and I are going to spend the day with my friend Serena and her kids somewhere safe."

Jaelyn squeezed her eyes closed and nodded. "Thank you."

"Any time." Ava gave her a one-armed hug, then turned. "Come on, guys, let's get out of here so Jaelyn and Adam can get on with what they have to do."

Missy held Leigha's hand and walked beside the seat, chattering away about singing songs together in the car.

"I'll be at the pharmacy once I see these guys safe." Jack hugged Jaelyn, then shook Adam's hand. "Don't worry, we've got this part. You two just get this done so that baby will be safe."

"Thank you, Jack." Adam clapped him on the back then watched them all climb into Jack's SUV and pull out of the driveway. Once they rounded the corner and were no longer in sight, he stepped back, guided Jaelyn back inside and closed the door. "Come on. The sooner we get this done, the sooner you'll be back with her."

She nodded.

"Jack and Ava brought breakfast sandwiches and coffee. Why don't you call the doctor and the pharmacy then we'll sit down for breakfast? You barely touched your food last night, and you need to eat something to keep up your strength."

"You're right." She patted his arm. "I'm okay, really. Just a little sad that the baby has to be going through all of this, that we had to traipse through the woods with her in the freezing cold rain…"

He gave in to the urge and pulled her close.

She buried her face against his chest and cried. "It hurts so much that a poor innocent child is in so much danger, that we may not be able to keep her safe, that Maya was so afraid for her life that she locked her in a closet and…"

He didn't know what to say, couldn't offer any reassurance, didn't dare utter the words she probably needed to hear—that everything would work out fine—because he had no idea if they were true.

She paused, stepped back from him.

"Why do you think Maya left her?" She turned to face the front door, seemed to look through it. "After only a couple of days I'm having a difficult time sending her with friends for a little while, and she's not even my child. What kind of danger do you think could have forced Maya to leave her alone?"

"I don't know." The thought of what would have happened to Leigha had they not found her had chased him in and out of nightmares since they'd found her. "The only thing I can figure is that she knew they'd found her, so she hid the baby and took off. Maybe she hoped they'd follow her and not search the room and find Leigha. I have to wonder if she planned to lose them and make it back to the bed and breakfast, or she assumed someone would hear her crying and investigate. Just because I didn't know she'd checked in with a baby doesn't mean the owner of the bed and breakfast didn't know."

She nodded, sucked in a shaky breath. "You're right. Sure. Maybe she figured the owner would hear her crying."

He rubbed a circle on her back, soothing himself as much as her. While he wanted as badly as she did to believe that was true, he just couldn't wrap his head around it. Maya had obviously gone to great lengths to keep the baby a secret. "Come on. Let's make these calls and eat something so we can get out of here."

His gaze fell on the Christmas tree he'd bought the

night before, and a sense of sadness descended. Suddenly, he wanted to be anywhere else but that cold, dreary room.

# TEN

Jaelyn counted slowly as she inhaled, held the breath for another count, then steadily exhaled. She sat in the driver's seat in a random parking lot a few miles from the pharmacy, Adam at her side. Gabe had provided a borrowed SUV, and Jaelyn sat behind the wheel, her hands slicked with sweat.

Everyone had told her she didn't have to go through with this—rather insistently. Gabe said they could have a police officer impersonate her sister, but they had none who shared Maya's same slim build and dark hair. If anyone who knew her was watching, they'd make out the undercover officer in an instant and back off.

So, Jaelyn had insisted on going. It was her plan, after all, and she was going to see it through.

"Jaelyn…" Adam brushed her hair back from her face and tilted his head to study her. If the deep lines marring his handsome features were any indication, he didn't like whatever it was he saw.

"Please, don't say it, Adam." If one more person asked if she was sure she wanted to do this, she just might run screaming for the hills.

"Okay, but you know I'll be close, and you remember what to do, right?"

She lifted a brow at him. "Park in the middle of the lot with easy access to an exit, walk briskly, but not too rushed, without looking around. If I make it inside, lower my sunglasses a little to show my face as if I'm searching for something before putting them back in place, then go straight to the counter. And do all of it while ignoring the giant bull's-eye painted on my back."

He shot her a grin. "Yup. That's it in a nutshell."

She had the plan down pat. That part wasn't the problem. The real problem was knowing that somewhere along the way, her plan would most likely be thwarted by an attempt to kidnap or kill her. Hopefully, the officers Gabe had stationed all over would be able to prevent them from succeeding.

*Ah, God, please walk with me through this. Help me save my sister and her child. Let Adam find the justice he so badly needs for his wife and unborn child so he might begin to heal.*

And what about her? Would she ever heal from having her life completely upended? Probably. Unless Maya walked away with Leigha and didn't allow Jaelyn to be a part of her life. Well, she'd just have to make sure that didn't happen, make sure Maya understood she wanted to get to know her better, wanted to understand the decisions she'd made, wanted to develop the relationship they'd been denied their whole lives. A twin. She still couldn't believe it.

"By the way, I heard from Carrie again this morning—

my paralegal—and apparently you own a ranch in Montana."

Jaelyn laughed out loud. Whatever she'd been expecting him to say, that had not been it. "So, what do you say when this is all over, we take a vacation?"

The words were out of her mouth before she even realized what she was going to say. She winced, wishing she could take them back and refusing to examine what part of her subconscious had betrayed her so completely.

"And not only that, you also have a valid Montana driver's license, from everything she could dig up. Not a forgery as I suspected."

Caught somewhere between embarrassment that she'd invited him on vacation and disappointment that he'd ignored it, she turned her head to look out the windshield. "Huh…what do you know?"

Adam must have sensed her discomfort, because he reached for her hand, which only made matters worse, so she slid it away to brush her hair behind her ear before he could take hold.

"Jaelyn, please. It's not that I don't feel… I don't know what…but something for you. It's just…if we had met at another time…under other circumstances… If… maybe before…" He slouched back into the soft leather seat, stared down at his hands in his lap as if they held the answers he sought.

She wanted to say something—anything—but no words came. What could she say to him?

"I'm damaged, Jaelyn. When Alessandra died, and our child with her, a part of me died with them. Alessandra was my world. She stood by me, encouraged me to pursue the case against the senator, actively involved herself in my investigation… She was strong and brave and loyal, and it got her killed." He paused as he battled to control his emotions.

Jaelyn tried to put herself in his place. When Ronnie betrayed her, she'd been able to hold onto anger at him, and that helped to ease some of the worst heartbreak. But Alessandra had been Adam's world, and she'd done nothing wrong to him. Quite the opposite, she'd been more than supportive. And she'd been ripped away from him.

"Please, Jaelyn, understand," he went on. "I care about you, and if we'd met at a different point in my life, it might have been something more. Maybe we could have gone on vacation together. Maybe we could've had lots of vacations together. You're an amazing person, an incredibly beautiful and kind person. I just can't ever allow myself to feel that strongly for anyone again." He looked at her, and the struggle was plain in his eyes. "As it is, I'd like to keep in touch when this is all over, maybe be friends. And for me, that's more of a commitment than I've made to any other person in the past five years, and it's all I have to give. Can you understand?"

Could she? Yes, actually. And hearing him say it put all of her feelings into perspective. She breathed a sigh of relief. The heightened emotions running through her were clouding her judgment. He'd touched something deep inside her that was better left alone. When this was done, she had to work on her relationship with her sister, work on building a relationship with her niece whom she'd already come to love, work on resolving the feeling of betrayal about her parents.

She lay her hand on the console between them, palm up. "I'd like to be friends when this is done, Adam. Like you, I have my own baggage to deal with before I could even think about being something to anyone else. When I said let's go on vacation, it wasn't an invitation to further our relationship, just a knee jerk reaction to escape the reality of our current situation." She grinned, hoping to lighten the mood.

He smiled at her, closed his hand over hers. "Well, that makes perfect sense."

Relieved the awkward moments had passed, she squeezed his hand, then glanced at the dashboard clock and sat up straighter.

A voice in the earpiece Gabe had insisted she wear told her they were ready to go. "It's time."

"Be careful, Jaelyn, and if anything at all seems off—"

"Don't worry." She offered him a genuine smile. "I'm really just a big chicken at heart. If something seems off, I'm outta there."

He reached for the door handle, hesitated. A variety of expressions ran over his features before his jaw clenched, his eyes hardened, and he opened the door and got out.

Pushing all thoughts of Adam out of her mind, knowing he'd be safe sitting in the parking lot with Pat and Jack, who'd returned after dropping Ava, Missy, and Leigha off with their friend, Jaelyn drove the few miles to the pharmacy. She kept watch for a tail.

Her emotions battled each other within her. Anticipation, fear, acceptance, all vying for the uppermost position in her thoughts. She quelled them all. She'd learned while fighting fires, going on rescue missions, how to detach herself from her emotions. It was more beneficial to react from a place of logic than of feelings. And so, she forced all of her feelings into a box and buried it deep, put every ounce of her focus into what she was about to do.

She scanned the lot as she pulled in, double-checked each of the officers was where they were supposed to be. She hadn't anticipated the crowd. She should have, the day after Christmas when they'd closed early on Christmas Eve and completely on Christmas Day.

She shoved that thought aside as well. The officers would work to keep everyone safe, and since this was like work, she had to trust them to do their jobs properly so she could focus on her part.

She backed into a parking spot toward the far end of the lot, close to the exit, as she expected Maya would probably do under the same circumstances, knowing she might have to escape in a hurry. Was that what she'd done at the bed and breakfast? Escaped in a hurry, been forced to go on the run without having time to implement whatever plan she may have had in place for Leigha?

She couldn't answer that question, and it would distract her when she needed to concentrate. She scanned the lot again, then emerged from the car, shifted her dark sunglasses tighter against her face. What would Maya do now? Would she linger, search for potential trouble? Or would she cross the lot with her head lifted and determination in her stride? Jaelyn had no idea, because the woman was a complete stranger to her.

A voice in her ear prodded her to move. She recognized the detective who'd helped Gabe set this up. She didn't acknowledge his order to start walking, simply started forward, adding a bit of confidence she didn't feel to her walk just in case whoever might be watching knew Maya better than Jaelyn did. Sweat dripped down her back, despite the near-freezing temperature. Though she'd worn dress slacks paired with a bulletproof vest beneath a winter coat, she'd drawn the line at the high heels Maya seemed to favor, opting instead for a low boot she could run in if necessary.

She was more than halfway across the lot and convinced their plan was doomed to fail when a tingle began at the base of her neck and slithered upward. The feeling of being watched overwhelmed her, nearly had her turning on her heel and running. Instead, she kept moving forward, staring straight at the front door, her expression neutral. She was bait, nothing more. Her role was to lure their pursuers into the open so the police could apprehend, then get out of the way as quickly as possible.

She clutched her purse with a fake ID in Maya's name against her chest, just in case she had to go inside and actually pick up the medication. Her breath came in shallow gasps that burned her lungs, a small waft of steam escaping with each forced exhalation. She was almost through the lot—just had to cross the lane between the pharmacy and the parking lot and she'd be on the sidewalk and entering the building. Torn between wanting something to happen, needing for all of this to end, and hoping no one would attack her, she almost missed the squeal of tires as a black sedan skidded into the lot, fishtailed around the first row of cars, and barreled toward her.

Jaelyn froze as the world erupted in her ears. "Go, go, go!"

Then someone slammed into her from the side, shoved her down between the cars and covered her head as gunfire shattered windows and car alarms wailed. Screams, cries, pounding footsteps, shouts and more gunfire ricocheted around the parking lot.

And then silence descended. For just an instant, there was no sound at all, like a vacuum had sucked her in, and the rest of the world sat suspended in time for that one moment.

"Jaelyn, are you hurt?" Gabe crouched beside her, glanced over his shoulder, then returned his attention to her. "Are you all right?"

"I am, yes." She assessed. A scraped knee, her heart racing like she'd just run a marathon, and the slacks she had on were torn and covered in wet gravel. She could live with that. "I'm fine. Did you guys get them?"

He pressed a hand against his ear, lowered his head for a moment.

She held her breath, waited, strained to hear the conversation through his earpiece, but couldn't make out anything but a sense of urgency.

Then he stood, held a hand out to her, and grinned. "We did. We got them. Both of them."

Instead of reaching for his hand, Jaelyn sat on the ice-cold blacktop, rested her back against the nearest car, which had an alarm blaring at full volume, and closed her eyes. They'd done it. If the men they'd apprehended answered their questions, this could all be over within the next couple of days. Leigha would be safe, Maya would be safe, Jaelyn and Adam could return to their... With suspects in custody who might well testify against Hunter Barlowe and Senator Lowell in order to save themselves, Adam would return to New York City and resume his life...alone.

Her heart ached for him, for the pain he'd already suffered. It would probably be difficult for him to go home to the silence without having the fight for justice to keep him from having to deal with the worst of the pain. Perhaps that pain would come now. Or perhaps he would heal. She truly prayed it would be the latter.

She sensed Gabe ease away, which was good. She needed some space, needed to breathe deep breaths of cool air. And she really needed to get this bulletproof vest off. Who knew it would be so heavy and cumbersome? She opened her eyes, and Adam was there, crouched in front of her.

He smiled. "We got them. Thank you, Jaelyn."

"Any time." A feeling of peace overtook her, the sense that everything had fallen into place. Not that they had all the answers they needed yet, but they were at least headed in the right direction. The two men they'd arrested for coming after Jaelyn would be questioned, and hopefully they'd talk, rattle off a list of names in exchange for a lesser sentence. Did that bother her? Not really. They needed the people at the top, Hunter Barlowe and Senator Lowell, or the two of them would just keep coming, or keep sending goons.

The joyful peace she'd been enjoying turned icy cold. What if they couldn't get the men to talk, to give up their employers?

"Hey." Adam reached out, tugged her hair in a friendly gesture she'd miss. "You all right?"

"Yes, I was…" She didn't want to spoil his good mood, but at the same time, were any of them really safe yet? "I was just thinking…"

"Don't worry about it. I'm going in with Gabe to observe the questioning once the two of them are processed. I'm figuring they'll talk right about the time they realize the severity of the charges that will be brought against them. Hopefully, we'll get enough information out of them to arrest and charge the senator and Hunter Barlowe."

"All right, then. I'll come with you. Will they let me observe?"

"Actually…" He held out a hand and helped her up. "You have somewhere else to be."

"Oh?" She quirked a brow at him. Where could he possibly think she'd rather be than seeing this through?

"Maya woke up. She's asking for you."

Adam walked her to Pat's SUV. He'd go with Jack to the police station, and Pat would take Jaelyn to the hospital. As much as he wanted to go with her, to offer his support while she spoke to her sister for the first time and hear what Maya had to say, he needed to follow up on the two men they'd just arrested. It would take a little while to get them processed and into an interrogation room, but in a town as small as Seaport, it probably wouldn't take long enough for him to go to the hospital with Jaelyn first.

He opened the car door for her. "I'll meet you at the hospital as soon as I'm done."

"Sure. That'd be good." She nodded but avoided his gaze.

"Hey."

She paused, glanced at him before climbing into the front seat beside Pat.

"I'm sure it's going to be fine. You and Maya certainly have a lot to talk about, a lot to say to one another. The other questions can wait." Hopefully until he got there, at least.

"You'll come, though? Because if you're sure, I'll wait for you to ask her about testifying against her husband and the senator."

He cradled her cheek in his hand, kissed her forehead. "I'll be there as soon as I can."

"Okay. I'll see you later."

He watched Pat drive away, saw Jaelyn glance in the side-view mirror, and waved. Although he second-guessed himself about a million times, envisioned himself running after the SUV and yelling for Pat to stop and wait for him, he had to see this through. He knew more about the situation with the Hunter than anyone in the department, and even though he'd brought the small task force Gabe had assembled up to speed on the major points, they could well miss something Adam might catch. Besides, Gabe had a patrol car following them, and there would be officers stationed outside the hospital room door. If anyone tried to get in, they'd be stopped.

They couldn't afford to botch this. If they did, Jaelyn might spend the rest of her life looking over her shoulder. Besides, she and her sister should be able to have some privacy to meet and get to know each other before he gave Maya the third degree and tried to convince her to turn against her husband and father.

Everything in him stilled. What if Maya told Jaelyn the truth about the senator being her father? Did Maya even know? All right, so he probably should have thought of that before sending Jaelyn off on her own to meet with her sister.

"Hey, man." Jack clapped a hand against his shoulder. "You gonna stand there all day, or do you want to head into the police station?"

"Oh, sorry." He shook off any misgivings. For all he knew, Maya didn't know who her father was any more than Jaelyn did. But the chance of that was slim—Maya knew about the adoption, and her husband worked closely with the senator. If she told Jaelyn who their father was, well…he'd just have to deal with that when the time came. But one thing was for certain, as soon as he got to the hospital and had a moment alone with Jaelyn, he was going to tell her the truth.

He hopped into the passenger seat of Jack's SUV. "Thanks for seeing this through, and for hanging around and giving me a ride."

"No problem. How are you doing? Okay?"

"Yeah, just wiped out." Wasn't that the understatement of the century. He couldn't remember the last decent night's sleep he'd had. Plus the physical activity, escaping from their pursuers, had used muscles he didn't even know he had. He needed to rest. And he needed to be able to go to the cemetery and tell Alessandra they'd finally stopped Senator Lowell.

He rolled his shoulders, tilted his head back and forth to ease the stiffness in his neck from sleeping on the couch all night. "Have you heard from Gabe?"

Jack looked in the rearview mirror and hit the turn signal then headed toward the police station. "Yeah, he called right before you got in the car and said neither of the two gunmen had any form of ID on them."

"What about the car? It had to have been registered to someone." Though he doubted Hunter Barlowe or Senator Lowell would be foolish enough to have registered it in their names.

"He didn't say. I'm sure they'll figure it out."

*Yeah, but would they?* No matter what obstacles got thrown into Senator Lowell's path, he seemed to be able to overcome them. Every time Adam had found someone who was willing to say the senator was responsible for blackmail, bribery, or intimidation, they either suddenly backed out of testifying or they disappeared. The senator was shrewd, knew how to manipulate people, maneuver them in the most painful way possible into doing exactly what he wanted them to do.

When Adam had gone after him, he hadn't killed Adam to stop him, and that would have been an option. A good option. But what pain would it have inflicted on him? None. So what had he done instead?

He'd gone after Adam's family, killed them to hurt him. And he was apparently arrogant enough to think he'd covered his tracks well enough that when Adam made it his mission in life to stop him, he'd still walk away free and clear.

Well, not this time. As long as Adam had breath in his body, he'd keep coming until he'd taken the man and his supporters down. And then...

And then what? Where did he go from there, once he could go to his wife and assure her Lowell was behind bars and would never hurt anyone else? What kind of life would he have? He'd been so caught up in seeking justice, so obsessed with his mission, he hadn't given any thought to what would come next.

The jolt of pain came hard and strong, pierced his heart with its jagged edge. Because once his vendetta was over, once his goal was achieved, he'd have nothing of Alessandra and his child left to hold on to. They would forever be a part of his past. And his future? His future was an endless expanse of emptiness.

Jack's phone rang, and Adam shut down his current line of thinking. It didn't matter right now. All that mattered was putting an end to Senator Lowell's reign of terror.

"It's Gabe." Jack hit a button on the dashboard screen and answered on his Bluetooth. "Hey, what's up?"

"Is Adam with you?"

Jack glanced over at him and frowned. "Yeah. Is anything wrong?"

"I just wanted to let him know we fingerprinted the two gunmen, and their prints aren't on file anywhere.

We're running a facial recognition program, but the tech isn't optimistic."

"So, no ID, no fingerprints on file for any reason?" Jack asked.

"Nope, nada. It's as if these two don't even exist."

How was that possible? Everyone left some kind of paper trail nowadays. It was early, and they hadn't had time to do much more than start a preliminary search, but still... "What about the car they were driving?"

"A guy paid cash for it last month from a seemingly random stranger who'd left it in the train station parking lot in Ronkonkoma with a For Sale sign in the window. The tags were stolen from a black sedan of the same make and model."

"No way that can all be coincidence." Adam's mind raced. They had to get something, anything from those men. It was their only lead. Without any kind of connection, the Hunter and the senator would go unpunished... again.

"No, I wouldn't think so." The call started to cut in and out.

And there was one thing Adam needed to know before it dropped. "Hey, Gabe, did you get a chance to question them yet?"

"Not officially, but I can tell you...not a word...not even...for a lawyer."

With the connection pretty much lost, Jack let Gabe know they'd be there in about fifteen minutes and then disconnected. "What do you make of it?"

Adam massaged his temples where a dull throb pulsed. "Honestly, I'm not surprised."

Senator Lowell was a master at covering his tracks, and he'd expect nothing less from those in his employ. And Hunter Barlowe was a tech genius and a cybersecurity wizard. Perhaps he handled more for the senator than just killings.

But something was nagging at him. A niggle at the base of his spine was urging him to figure it out. He was missing something important. There were too many questions, not enough answers. He'd been hoping the two gunmen they had in custody would provide at least some of those answers. He needed to be at the police station, needed to hear what they had to say.

How had Lowell managed to erase any sign the two men ever existed? Did they even work for him? Or had Hunter Barlowe hired them? As a cybersecurity expert, he'd surely be able to hack and delete any records.

A jolt of terror rocketed through him. "Stop the car."

Jack hit the brakes and pulled to the curb even as he frowned at Adam. "What's wrong?"

"Was Pat going to stay with Jaelyn at the hospital?"

He was already shaking his head. "She wanted to talk to Maya alone, said she'd be fine. And there are officers posted at the hospital."

"Go to the hospital." He couldn't explain why, but he had a strong feeling he needed to get to Jaelyn.

"What? Why?" Jack hit the turn signal, looked over his shoulder, and swung a U-turn.

"It doesn't make sense for Senator Lowell to have sent anyone after Maya or Jaelyn." Or did it? He'd obviously paid for the hit on Jaelyn's parents. Had he had Maya's parents killed too? For what purpose? Unless the hit list was a fake. Maybe Hunter was setting the senator up. Once Adam had discovered the list with the senator's initials after so many hits, he'd gotten distracted, lost focus, shifted his attention to the senator as the ringleader. And yet… "It makes more sense to me that it's Maya's husband, Hunter Barlowe, the hitman known as the Hunter, who's been trying to get at her. And now she and Jaelyn are alone in that hospital room."

# ELEVEN

Jaelyn stood outside Maya's door. She'd sent Pat home. There were police officers down the hall, and Pat had already missed enough of the holidays with his family because he was helping her. Besides, she needed a few minutes to collect herself before meeting her sister for the first time. What did you say to the twin you never knew existed? Should she introduce herself? That seemed weird, considering Maya already knew who she was.

Enough worrying already. Surely she'd figure out the right thing to say when she came face-to-face with the woman whose child she'd already come to care so much for. Whatever was said now, she prayed Maya would allow her to remain a part of Leigha's life.

She blew out a breath and eased the door open, peeked her head into the room.

Maya was sitting up in the bed, staring toward the window where the blinds had been drawn closed.

"Maya?"

She turned her head to face Jaelyn and reached out a hand. "Thank you for coming."

"Of course." Jaelyn crossed the room to her, gripped

her hand. The resemblance was incredible, like looking into a mirror. It was definitely going to take some getting used to. "How are you?"

"I'm okay, thank you, but there's something I have to ask you." Her eyes were swollen, red-rimmed, as if she'd spent hours crying.

"Of course."

Pain twisted her features; tear tracks stained her cheeks. "I left something in the closet at the bed and breakfast where—"

"She's fine." Jaelyn caught Maya's hand in both of hers and kept her voice low. "I have her."

"Oh, thank you." She dropped back against the pillows, squeezed her eyes closed. "I was worried sick. I'd made arrangements for someone to pick her up if he didn't hear from me by a certain time, but when he got there, she was already gone. He was able to find out you'd been there, in my room, but I didn't know if you'd been the one to take Leigha."

The fact that Maya had made arrangements for someone to get Leigha brought an instant sense of relief. She still had a million questions, like why she'd gone on the run, but the most important one in Jaelyn's mind had been answered. She hadn't abandoned her child, only hidden her to keep her safe. "I'm sorry, Maya. I wasn't sure what to do when I found her there, but I couldn't leave her when one of the men trying to find you was already in the room."

"No, no. Please, you did the right thing. Thank you. If you hadn't…" She shivered and sat up straighter. "Well, I don't even want to think about what might have happened if someone else had gotten to her before my guy did."

With that out of the way, Jaelyn didn't know where to start. There was so much she wanted to know. Who were their birth parents? Where were they now? Had Maya known about Jaelyn all along? What kind of trouble was she in, and how could Jaelyn help?

"Where is Leigha now?" Maya tucked her free hand beneath the blanket. "I need you to take me to her."

Keeping Maya's hand in hers, Jaelyn sat beside her on the edge of the bed. She could certainly understand Maya's desperation to see Leigha, but she was in no condition to leave the hospital. Instead, Jaelyn would bring the baby to her. "I don't think they'll release you yet, considering your injuries."

She yanked her hand from Jaelyn's. "I'm getting out of here and going to my daughter. Now."

The woman needed reassurance. "Okay, just hold on a sec. I understand how upset you must be and how desperate you must be to get to her, but I promise you she's safe. She's with friends of mine, friends I know I can trust to watch out for her. I can ask them to—"

Maya narrowed her gaze, and some of the warmth slid away to reveal a cold emptiness in her eyes. "What friends?"

A chill raced through Jaelyn. Why was Maya looking at her like that? Did she think Jaelyn would try to keep Leigha from her? She stood and reached for the button to call the nurse before Maya could get any more upset, or worse, pull the IV line out on her own.

"I said…" Maya lifted her other hand from beneath

the blanket and aimed a handgun with an attached silencer at Jaelyn. "What friends?"

Jaelyn gasped. Her hand froze midway to the call button. "Where did you get the gun?"

"My guy wasn't only responsible for retrieving Leigha. He monitored me and brought it as soon as I woke up." Maya grabbed her wrist, and when Jaelyn tried to pull away from her, she maintained an iron grip.

"What's going on, Maya? I wasn't trying to keep her from you. I just wanted to keep her safe from whoever was after us until you recovered. I was going to ask my friends to bring her here to you."

"Well, I'm recovered enough, so you and I are going to get out of here and go get my daughter." She spoke with a deadly calm. "Then you're going to give me the briefcase and diaper bag you swiped from my room, the briefcase I took a beating from the senator's men to keep hidden, and I'm going to disappear. Now, step back. And don't you dare breathe a word about the gun to anyone, or you will die." She released Jaelyn's hand, threw the covers off, and swung her feet off the bed, all while keeping the gun steady. "The only reason you're still breathing right now is because you have that child. If not for her, you'd already be dead in this bed, and I'd be taking your place."

What was she talking about? The senator was after Maya? But deep in her heart, Jaelyn suspected she already knew that. "The guy who attacked me when I went to your room at the bed and breakfast, he belonged to the senator?"

"Yes, seems Senator Lowell wasn't happy when I took off."

So it wasn't her husband who'd been hunting her down. "And the guys who killed the senator's man, the same ones who tried to kill me at the safe house, they didn't belong to the senator, did they? They belonged to you."

"Good to see smart runs in the family." It all came crashing down on Jaelyn—all this time, they'd been hunted by two sets of bad guys. The senator's men after Maya, and Maya's guys after her. "Now, let's go."

Could she stall Maya? What would the woman do if someone came in? Adam had said he'd meet her here. Maybe she could keep Maya talking long enough for him to show up. But then what? She didn't want to put him in danger. But she did want him, desperately. She wanted him to cocoon her in his arms as he had on the beach, she wanted the chance to tell him she'd been wrong, that she did have feelings for him. Very strong feelings that scared her half to death. "You wouldn't get away with switching places with me," Jaelyn said. "People would know it was me, not you, who died."

She shrugged. "Maybe, but it wouldn't matter. You'd have been beaten as severely as I was and left in the bed. If anyone had reason to suspect it wasn't me, they'd run into a problem identifying the corpse since all records of my existence have already been wiped. And soon yours will be wiped as well and replaced with those I've forged before I leave for Montana, where I'll start a new life with my husband and child as Jaelyn Reed."

"Your husband?" Jaelyn's blood ran cold. If she was

going on the run with Hunter Barlowe, with all of the documents she had in her possession, then she had to know who and what he was and must be okay with it. Jaelyn didn't know why that surprised her, especially knowing Maya had already sent men to kill her.

She had to think. She was in trouble—real trouble.

Already dressed, Maya stood and slid her feet into her shoes. "You and I are going to walk out of here. You will smile, nod, say you're taking me for a walk to stretch my legs, say or do whatever it takes to get me out of this hospital without anyone stopping me. Do you understand?"

She simply nodded, since her mouth had gone too dry to speak. She'd go along, cooperate with Maya for now, until she could find a way to take her out.

Maya yanked the tape from her arm and the IV, which she'd already removed, came free. She gestured toward the door with the weapon. "Walk."

Jaelyn turned toward the door, struggled to ignore the wave of emotions threatening to drown her so she could think clearly.

Maya came up beside her, gripped her elbow. She held the weapon in her other hand, secreted in her pocket, no doubt aimed at Jaelyn. "I will not hesitate to kill anyone who tries to stop me. You included."

At her nod, Jaelyn opened the door. Her heart raced frantically, her pulse pounding in her ears. All she had to do was walk out. They just had to make it into the elevator at the end of the hallway and then out of the hospital. And then what?

"Where are we going?" Jaelyn let Maya set the pace,

which was not nearly as slow as Jaelyn would have expected, considering her injuries.

When they reached the elevator doors, Maya stopped. "First floor."

Jaelyn pushed the button, waited. So many things flew through her mind. Leigha. How could she send that innocent child off with this woman and her hitman husband? How could she bring this woman to Ava and her little girl after they'd been so kind and taken her daughter in? Would she kill them as well? She'd have to, wouldn't she? She couldn't leave any witnesses.

The ding of the elevator arriving pulled her back to the moment.

Maya smiled at an elderly gentleman emerging then guided Jaelyn inside.

Jaelyn held her breath while the doors closed, praying no one else would get on with them. When the doors finally shut, she asked again, "Where are we going?"

"We're going to pick up my daughter, and then my family and I will be leaving for our ranch in Montana."

"If you're in trouble, Maya, I can help you. You don't have to do this. I have friends who can keep you and Leigha safe."

"Oh, do you now?" She scoffed. "Safe from whom exactly?"

How much should she say? Should she admit to knowing the truth about her husband? What did she really have to lose at this point? Since there was no way she could bring Maya to Ava's, Jaelyn was already as good as dead. "I know about your husband. I know Hunter Barlowe is the hitman known as the Hunter."

Maya laughed out loud, a deep rocking laugh that had tears running down her cheeks. "Oh, honey, you know nothing. My husband isn't the Hunter."

"But I saw the documents with the hit list, the amounts paid…my parents' names."

"Oh, right, sorry about that." The elevator doors slid open, and Maya yanked her out into the busy lobby. No one seemed to notice the two women passing through. "But that one's not on me. That was dear old Dad who insisted the Hunter get rid of them."

"Dad? What are you talking about?"

Maya crossed over the threshold and onto the sidewalk, then stepped to the side and stopped. She looked Jaelyn straight in the eye. "Our real father, Senator Lowell, hired the Hunter to kill your adoptive parents so they would be out of the way before he runs for president. Anyone who knew the truth about us, that his mistress gave birth to us and put us up for adoption, had to be eliminated. Just as our mother was eliminated right after we were born. He'd have killed you too, had people tailing you and everything, but when he realized you never knew you were adopted he developed a soft spot and let you live."

She spat the words with such bitterness, such jealousy, Jaelyn almost felt sorry for her.

Jaelyn's head spun, not because she couldn't wrap her head around the whole situation, but because it made a sick sort of sense. "How do you know all of this if your husband isn't the Hunter?"

"Because, dear, my husband, Hunter Barlowe, met his end years ago, once he'd served his purpose and was no longer needed to keep up appearances. Since then, he's only existed on paper, a persona I created to take the fall when I decided to retire. I'm the Hunter."

Adam spotted Jaelyn and Maya standing on the curb when Jack pulled up. "What are they doing out here?"

Jack looked in the direction he indicated then shifted into park. "Do you want me to wait here?"

"Yeah, would you mind? Just give me a minute to find out what's going on?"

"Sure, man, no problem."

Adam hopped out of the SUV and started toward Jaelyn.

The instant she spotted him, she stiffened. She cast a glance toward Maya then shook her head once.

He paused, glanced back to where Jack still sat watching him from the SUV, then back at Jaelyn. Something was wrong.

A Jeep pulled up to the curb, and Maya kept hold of Jaelyn's elbow as she urged her forward.

Adam ran back to Jack. "I don't know what's going on, but call Gabe and follow that Jeep without letting them know they're being followed."

He didn't wait for an answer, hoped Jack would do as he'd asked, but no way was that woman getting Jaelyn into that vehicle alone. He forced a smile and waved as he hurried toward them. "Jaelyn, hey, hold up."

Thankfully, Maya averted her gaze and didn't see him, probably not wanting to have to stop and explain why there were suddenly two Jaelyns.

Jaelyn stopped, waved back. "Hey there…uh, sorry

I don't have time to chat right now. My sister just got released from the hospital, and I'm taking her home."

Sweat beaded on her forehead; despite the chill in the air, it snaked along her hairline. Though she'd schooled her expression, she couldn't hide the sheer terror in her eyes.

"That's okay." He moved closer, was almost within reach of her. "I won't keep you long, I just had a quick question."

The man driving the Jeep reached across the passenger seat and shoved the door open. "You're going to have to take him too, Maya."

Adam's heart stopped. "Josiah?"

"Climb into the back seat." Maya nodded toward the Jeep. "Now. Or I kill her."

He did as she said. Then, with his full attention focused on the dead man in the driver's seat, he slid across so Jaelyn could climb in next to him. "I don't understand. How are you alive? I watched you die."

"You saw what we wanted you to see." Maya slammed the door behind them, then climbed into the passenger seat and leaned across the console to kiss Josiah. "We faked Josiah's death so we could start our new life together in peace with no one the wiser. Drive, dear."

Rage poured through him. He'd shouldered the guilt for this man's death. "How?"

Josiah offered a cold smile in the rearview mirror. "Maya was the shooter, and the gun was loaded with blanks. I hit the blood pack under my shirt and then just played dead." He shifted into gear and started through the parking lot. "When she kept shooting, you had to run. Maya's associates picked me up and she hacked the medical examiner's office to close out my case, death from a gunshot wound to the chest. And there you have it. Josiah Cameron no longer exists."

All of the emotions he'd held at bay over the past years threatened to boil over. These people had no regard for anyone, simply manipulated whoever they had to in order to get their way. "But why come to me in the first place if you were going to fake your death all along?"

"Actually, that wasn't part of the original plan." Josiah's expression turned sour. "We had the whole thing set up so perfectly. We left enough circumstantial evidence to get me arrested so I could come to you and provide real evidence against the senator and then watch him burn. Just the thought of outwitting him, of watching him spend the rest of his life in prison knowing we were the ones to put him there, was joyous." He sighed. "The plan was for the senator to go down for hiring out the hits, for Hunter Barlowe to disappear and become the stuff of legends, and for us to find our happily ever after." He glanced at Maya next to him. "But it didn't work out that way. When Senator Lowell ordered a hit on me, we knew we could never find peace as long as he was alive. Or as long as we were." Josiah smiled, then turned his attention to the road ahead and pulled out. "Which way?"

"My dear sister was just about to tell me that, weren't you, Jaelyn?" Maya turned to point the gun at Adam between the seats.

"I'm sorry, Adam." Jaelyn slid her hand into his and

gripped it tightly. "Make a right when you leave the parking lot."

He forced the fury down. It would do neither of them any good. He had to get a grip on himself and stall, because there was no way he was watching the woman he felt so much more for than he'd been willing to admit die. He'd been a fool to ignore his feelings for her, to suppress them to keep from risking his heart again. Now he just had to live long enough to tell her he'd risk his heart or anything else for her, and ask her to take that same chance. "What's going on here, Jaelyn?"

Maya met Jaelyn's gaze and smirked. "Oh, feel free to fill him in. It's not like either of you are going to be talking to anyone else once we get where we're going."

Adam resisted the desperate urge to glance behind him to see if Jack was following. He had to trust the other man would get them help.

"It seems we were wrong about who the Hunter was." Jaelyn's voice shook wildly, and he wanted desperately to pull her into his arms, comfort her, shield her from danger. "Hunter Barlowe no longer exists. He's *her...* Maya is the Hunter."

His mind raced to put the pieces together. Once he did, his stomach sank. No wonder he'd never seen her with her husband. The man was already dead.

"But why, Maya? I don't understand," Jaelyn said.

"That's because you went to a loving family who doted on you and gave you the best of everything." The bitterness in her voice turned Adam's stomach and made him fear for Jaelyn even more. "I, on the other hand, went to Daddy's dear friend, the dear friend he liked so much, he had him killed the day I turned eighteen. At that time, he offered me his job."

"As a hired gun?" Jaelyn's voice had gone from terrified to shocked.

"Of course." Maya seemed to ponder something for a moment, then turned toward the front and met Jaelyn's eyes in the rearview mirror. "Come to think of it, that was probably his intention all along, to have me follow in my adoptive father's footsteps. He never trusted that man, not fully, and he had him start training me from the time I was old enough to handle a weapon. Then, as soon as I was trained and at a suitable age to take his place, he got rid of him."

Adam squeezed Jaelyn's hand, willing her to keep the other woman talking. If she shifted her gaze from Jaelyn, she might well spot Jack or a police officer behind them and kill Jaelyn here and now.

"So, why are you running now? Why are you stealing my life and going on the run?" Jaelyn asked.

"When I found out I was pregnant, I knew Lowell would never allow me to go off and live my life in peace. And if I killed a sitting senator, no matter how tempting, I would be hunted to the ends of the earth. While getting beat up by Daddy's thugs didn't factor into my plan, faking my own death after pretending to eliminate Josiah did. This way, Daddy Dearest thinks I'm dead, he thinks Josiah's dead and that I followed orders. And we're free to live our lives."

"But why take *my* life?" Jaelyn's voice lost all of the tremor, went icy cold. "You could be anyone."

"You're right, I could have invented any alias I wanted

and left you alone, but why should *you* have gotten the good life? Why did *you* get to grow up in a nice little town, with loving parents, friends…you probably even had a golden retriever, for crying out loud." Maya whirled on her, and the viciousness in her eyes had Jaelyn shrinking back and Adam going on alert.

The short burst of a police siren sounded from behind them, and Maya lifted her gaze out the back window.

Adam didn't turn around, didn't dare shift his attention from the irate woman sputtering in the front seat.

"What did you do?" she screamed and lifted the gun toward Jaelyn, her eyes filled with so much hatred Adam had no doubt she'd kill her.

He grabbed Maya's wrist, shoved her arm up, yanked his own weapon from the back of his jeans and pointed it at Josiah's head. "It's over, Maya. Don't move."

He couldn't help the tremor in the hand holding the gun. He wasn't afraid, but he was holding onto the woman who'd killed Alessandra and their child, the woman who'd tried to kill Jaelyn and Leigha. He had every reason in the world to shift his aim and end her here and now to ensure she never killed anyone else. And one very big reason not to. He forced his weapon to hold steady.

Josiah slammed on the brakes. The SUV skidded to an abrupt stop as he jammed it into Park, shoved the door open, and dove out.

With the threat to him removed, Maya lunged toward Adam, raked her razor sharp nails down the side of his face as she struggled to free her gun hand.

He jerked back, faltered his own weapon in a desperate attempt to hold onto her.

Before he could regain his hold on the gun, Jaelyn shifted onto one knee, grabbed the seat back and swung like a champion, landing a solid blow to Maya's chin.

Maya's eyes rolled up.

With his weapon recovered, Adam held it aimed at Maya and prayed she'd stop fighting. Because he didn't want to have to pull the trigger, didn't want to see her die at his hand. She'd go to court, as was her right, and hopefully be convicted not only for Alessandra and their child's murders, but for all the others she'd committed as well. And that would have to be enough. "Josiah?"

"The police have him." Jaelyn lay a hand on his arm. "It's over, Adam."

And, as police officers led by Gabe swarmed the vehicle and took Josiah and Maya into custody, he knew that Jaelyn was right. It finally was over.

He had to get out of the car, needed air. He shoved the Jeep door open and climbed out. Chaos surrounded him, but he ignored it all.

"Hey, man, you okay?" Jack lay a hand on his back.

Adam only nodded. In the moment he'd looked into Maya's eyes and knew she was about to pull the trigger, a realization had flooded through him. He loved Jaelyn with all his heart, couldn't be without her.

She slid into his arms, wrapped her arms around him, and lay her head against his chest.

"I love you, Jaelyn," he said. "I'm sorry I didn't realize sooner, didn't tell you—"

"You're telling me now. And I love you too, Adam."

She looked up at him and smiled, then stood on her tiptoes and pressed her lips to his.

And with that, the bleak future he'd envisioned suddenly seemed so much brighter.

# EPILOGUE

Jaelyn rocked lazily back and forth on the porch swing, Leigha snoring softly beside her, her head resting in Jaelyn's lap. She lay a hand on her still flat stomach where a new life grew, a life only she and Adam knew about for the moment. But soon it would be time to share their joy. She wasn't ready to tell anyone else yet, not until the trial was over and Maya's fate decided…and she would know very soon what that fate was. Adam had been on standby all day waiting to hear the verdict. So, there she sat on the wide wraparound porch of their new home in Seaport, the home they'd moved into after getting married four months earlier.

Suddenly Adam leaned over from behind her, wrapped his arms around her, and entwined his hands with hers over their child. "I bet I know what you're thinking about."

She laughed and leaned against him, the woodsy scent of his aftershave cocooning her in comfort and a feeling of safety. Over the past year, she'd suffered nightmares and hadn't slept well, but having Adam beside her these past months had helped tremendously, and she'd begun to heal. "Have you heard anything?"

"It's over, baby."

The trial had dragged on forever, and the verdict had been slow in coming.

"And?" Jaelyn held her breath. If Maya wasn't found guilty, wasn't convicted, what would they do? She looked down at Leigha, napping peacefully on the cushion next to her. No way was she giving this child back to that monster.

"She and Josiah were both found guilty of murder. Josiah for the guy in the bed and breakfast, and Maya for the whole list of people documented in her paperwork." He rounded the swing to sit on the other side of her with Leigha between them, tucked a few strands of hair that the gentle spring breeze had blown into her face behind her ear. "They are both going away for a very long time."

He put an arm around her, stroking Leigha's cheek. "And she's ours, Jaelyn. No one can take her from us now."

She sobbed softly, the pain of not knowing if they'd get to keep Leigha finally relieved. They'd been granted emergency custody. Maya had agreed to waive her parental rights so they could adopt her only if she was convicted. "The senator?"

"Maya's testimony assured he's done," Adam said.

She nodded, wiped her eyes, and leaned against her husband. She'd given Maya and Senator Lowell all the time she'd ever give them. Now, it was time to move on, time to live her life with her husband and children.

"And now that the trial's over," Adam continued, "all the forgeries in your name will be destroyed. The ranch is to be sold. Since it's in your name, I asked that the money be donated to an organization that helps abused women and children."

"That's fine. It's good. I have all I ever want from that woman." She lifted Leigha onto her lap, cuddled her as she scooted closer to Adam.

Adam shifted so he could look into her eyes. "Are you okay?"

"I am now." And with their children between them, she pressed her lips to his, then pulled back to look at him. "Everything is perfect now."

\* \* \* \* \*

*If you enjoyed*
Christmas in the Crosshairs
*by Deena Alexander*

*Be sure to check out*
Kidnapped in the Woods
*Available now from Love Inspired Suspense!*

*Discover more at LoveInspired.com*

Dear Reader,

Thank you so much for sharing Adam and Jaelyn's story! I love flawed characters whose internal conflicts are as unique and challenging as the danger they find themselves in.

One of the things both Adam and Jaelyn struggle with is the ability to trust. They've both been hurt in the past and are having a difficult time learning to trust again. I think all of us go through trials in our lives that make it difficult to open up and trust one another, but as long as we continue to trust in God, I believe we can learn to trust others again.

I hope you've enjoyed sharing Adam and Jaelyn's journey as much as I enjoyed creating it. If you'd like to keep up with my new stories, you can find me on Facebook, www.facebook.com/DeenaAlexanderAuthor, and on Twitter, @DeenaAlexanderA.

Or sign up for my newsletter, https://gmail.us10.list-manage.com/subscribe?u=d7e6e9ecdc0888d7324788ffc&id=42d52965df.

*Deena Alexander*

## TRACKING STOLEN TREASURES
*K-9 Search and Rescue* • by Lisa Phillips

On the trail of a vicious jewel-theft ring, FBI special agent Alena Sanchez is undercover at a medical conference when her prime suspect is kidnapped. Now she'll have to team up with K-9 officer Hank Miller to uncover how theft leads to cold-blooded murder.

## BURIED GRAVE SECRETS
*Crisis Rescue Team* • by Darlene L. Turner

When forensic anthropologist Jordyn Miller is targeted for discovering an unmarked graveyard, she knows someone is determined to keep old secrets buried. Constable Colt Peters and his K-9 protector dog are called in to guard her life—but exposing a serial killer could be the last thing they do...

## UNDERCOVER BABY RESCUE
by Maggie K. Black

To save his stolen nephew from a dangerous trafficking organization, Officer Justin Leacock will have to go undercover as a married couple with his former fiancée, Detective Violet Jones. But finding the boy isn't enough—they must outwit the kidnappers on their tail and survive the ruthless icy wilderness, too...

## MONTANA WITNESS CHASE
by Sharon Dunn

After testifying against her brother's murderer, Hope Miller is placed in witness protection—only to be attacked at her new safe house. With her identity compromised, it's up to US marshal Andrew Lewis to safeguard her. But stopping the crime ring could prove lethal for them both.

## DANGEROUS RANCH THREAT
by Karen Kirst

When rancher Cassie West discovers that several murder victims bear a striking resemblance to her, it's clear there's a serial killer at large... and she's the next target. Can she and her temporary ranch hand Luke McCoy expose the killer before they exact vengeance?

## HUNTED IN THE MOUNTAINS
by Addie Ellis

Pursued by assailants, a terrified child shows up at Julia Fay's door—and soon they're both running for their lives. Can Julia and former navy SEAL Troy Walker protect the boy against the unknown...when the truth could get them killed?

---

# Get 3 FREE REWARDS!

**We'll send you 2 FREE Books plus a FREE Mystery Gift.**

**FREE** Value Over **$20**

Both the **Love Inspired®** and **Love Inspired® Suspense** series feature compelling novels filled with inspirational romance, faith, forgiveness and hope.

# HARLEQUIN
## PLUS

Try the best multimedia
subscription service for romance
readers like you!

---

## Read, Watch and Play.

Experience the easiest way to get
the romance content you crave.

Start your **FREE TRIAL** at
<u>www.harlequinplus.com/freetrial</u>.